Feathers

of

Phoenix

Flame

By Kelly Rich

Book One of the Midlings Saga

For my wonderful husband, Nathan, who has supported me in every endeavor since day one. Every dream I've ever had come true has happened with you at my side.

Contact the author at author@kellyrichbooks.com

Cover design by bobooks

Table of Contents

Chapter One
The Voice Within

Breathe, Kieran. Breathe.

It was like another voice beside his own repeated the words over and over. The pressure on his back grew stronger and Kieran struggled to take a deep breath. He needed to push himself up from the ground, but his arms were tightly bound behind his back.

I'm caught! Kieran's heart pounded. Several guards from the Order of Peria surrounded Kieran. They wore white mages' robes with scarlet edging on the sleeves and hems. Unlike traditional guards, these were trained in the magical artes and knew how to subdue a magical offender.

Kieran couldn't rise to his feet to complete a wielding form, so the magic coursing through his veins proved useless at the moment. He looked ahead at the chaotic scene in the streets.

What happened? Kieran wondered, shivering as the chill wind ruffled his fiery red hair. His slender body shook, and he closed his green eyes.

Kieran's memory felt fuzzy, as did his vision, but as it came back into focus, he could see more members of the Order extinguishing flames. They wore robes of silvery blue and called forth water from a nearby well.

With sweeping flourishes of their hands, they directed the water at the remaining fires.

The water connected with the smoldering flames with a loud hiss and steam rose into the air. Finally, the last of the fires were put out and the members of the Order turned their attention back to Kieran.

"Kieran of Tarmuth, you are accused of wielding the arte of flame in a manner not in accordance with the laws of the Order of Peria."

Yeah, yeah, that's nothing new, Kieran thought stubbornly. He'd had twelve years worth of encounters with the city guards. He wriggled against his restraints, but they didn't loosen.

Kieran looked more closely at the guards surrounding him. The white robes with red markings were the traditional garb of Flamemasters. They wore their robes open in the front and pulled across their shoulders. Even in the cold winter's air they wore sleeveless tunics beneath their robes.

Bet they stay plenty warm on their own, Kieran mused to himself. It was hardly the time for amusement. However, being as it wasn't his first encounter with the Order, he wasn't particularly worried.

After a moment of scanning the looks of the gathered crowd, Kieran started to grow nervous. This time seemed different. The lingering smell of smoke still hung in the cold air and there were charred marks on many of the surrounding buildings. It was also odd to Kieran that he couldn't quite remember what had happened.

Kieran could recall watching the Sombrayn elves lighting the torches, as was customary each night. Several of them now stood vigil over him. He looked up at their thin elven faces. Most had dark, short hair and chestnut brown eyes.

The middle of winter had settled on Peria, bringing its biting winds and icy flurries. Without a solid roof over his head, Kieran stayed on the move in the city, stopping to draw in heat from the torches being lit.

Typically, the Order would issue a stern warning to Kieran about improperly using magic in the streets. Being restrained by six Flamemasters? Well, that was new.

Realization started to dawn on Kieran as the elves raised him to his feet.

"Wait, guys, you don't think I did this?" he stammered nervously. They stared back at him with stoic faces.

"I didn't start this fire!" Kieran shouted as the elves pushed him forward. He tried to dig in his heels but was easily overcome by his captors.

"Wait! This is a misunderstanding! I can't wield fire! I can only connect to the heat!"

One of the Sombrayns turned to Kieran. "You will have your chance to defend your actions at your hearing before the Keepers of the Order."

Kieran's pulse quickened. "The Keepers? No, no, no! There's no need for that! I didn't do this!"

Still, he was ignored. Kieran's palms grew sweaty and his mouth felt dry. He was starting to feel sick.

This is bad! Kieran thought to himself. *How do I get out of this mess?*

Onward they marched through the streets with Kieran dragging his feet. One of the Flamemasters kept giving him a firm tug to keep him walking. At last they reached a stone building. Kieran was ushered inside and led down a long hallway. One of the guards slipped a key into an iron door. Its hinges creaked ominously as it swung open.

The elves pushed Kieran inside and he nearly toppled over. As he regained his balance, he spun toward the door. Just before he could reach it, an elf slammed it shut. Kieran grabbed ahold of the iron bars and cried out. The elves ignored him and walked away. Two Flamemasters stayed nearby.

As his heart raced, Kieran turned around wildly in the room taking in his surroundings. Cold stone walls surrounded him on all sides except for the wall that held the large iron door. There were no windows to let in any outside light. The only object in the room was a thin straw mattress thrown hastily in a corner. The entire cell was lit with a soft, bluish light that radiated from the walls.

Moonstone, Kieran thought glumly. The land of Peria was rich in magic, more than just its inhabitants but in the very land itself. Moonstone was a natural source of illuminating magic, steady and unwavering. Moonstone could be worked and shaped into an object or used to build with, but the magical source itself did not yield to a mage's manipulation of it.

I can't use it to get out of here.

Kieran slumped down onto the lumpy mattress releasing a cloud of dust into the air. He groaned and laid back, trying to get comfortable. The mattress was so sparse Kieran might as well have laid on the floor.

After a couple of restless hours, Kieran stood back up and began pacing around the small cell. He watched as the first two guards were relieved by a single Flamemaster. Curious, Kieran leaned against the wall near the door to get a better look.

This Flamemaster was another strong, Sombrayn elf. His hair fell neatly to the left and his strong posture gave an air of authority. His white and scarlet robe was crisp and without a wrinkle. Even in the weak glow of moonstone, his polished black boots shone.

Well, he must be someone important, Kieran thought.

The elf stood resolutely outside the door to the cell, paying Kieran no attention. Kieran bored with watching him, so he turned away.

A dark shadow on the wall where he had been leaning caught Kieran's attention. He looked closely at the Moonstone. Whereas most of the room still had the faint bluish glow, there was a perfect dark handprint where Kieran had touched.

Intrigued, Kieran placed his hands on the wall again where the Moonstone readily glowed. After a moment he pulled his hands away, revealing two more dark handprints.

How is this possible? Kieran wondered.

Moonstone is usually not affected by a mage.

Kieran could barely apply the term mage to himself. While most everyone in the land of Peria was capable of magic, those left untrained were not allowed to refer to themselves as mages. Kieran had felt the stirrings since he was a boy, but without parents or anyone else close to him, he was left to learn magic on his own. He would draw close to anyone speaking about magic, eagerly soaking up any tidbits of wisdom that were offered. That was how he learned of Moonstone and its properties.

Now Kieran was left confused, but with an idea. Moving to the center of the wall, he placed his hands once again against the stone. Closing his eyes, he began to draw in the Moonstone's energy. Slowly the light began to fade from the cell until it was plunged into sudden darkness.

A scuffling sound came from the Sombrayn outside the cell. Kieran sank into the dark corner and watched as the Flamemaster called forth a bright orb of fire. He lifted it into the air and scanned the cell.

Kieran scrunched down further in the corner and held his breath. The clink of a metal key inside the iron lock made his heart soar. He readied himself as the Sombrayn stepped inside.

Kieran bolted from the corner with a yell, startling the Sombrayn. He leapt for the open door and dashed into the hallway. However, before he could get very far at all, the Sombrayn elf cast out flames. They blazed past Kieran and trapped him in the center of a fiery circle.

In a moment of panic, Kieran reached out to connect to the flame in an attempt to control it. As his own magic made contact with the elf's, a feathery spark shot out from Kieran. It danced before his eyes for just a moment before dissipating into shining embers.

That's never happened before! Kieran thought in amazement. The elf also looked rather surprised, but continued to hold the wall of flames around Kieran.

Knowing he could not compete with a trained Flamemaster, Kieran threw up his hands in submission to the wielder. The elf's flames illuminated his face and Kieran could make out a small, crescent-shaped scar on his left cheek. Unlike most of the other Sombrayn elves, this man had green eyes, much like Kieran's own.

The elf called out for reinforcements that quickly came. Once again, Kieran's hands were subdued. He was roughly tossed back inside the cell. The guards talked tensely among themselves.

"Are you hurt, Flamemaster Caydn?" a guard asked. Kieran noted the scarred elf's name.

"I am well," Caydn replied in a deep voice. He glanced at Kieran with a stern look.

"Perhaps his magic should be suppressed," one of the others remarked.

Kieran tensed. Suppression of one's magic was an extreme measure that would render someone incapable of using magic for a time.

Caydn was firm. "He's just a child. The Order forbids such force against one so young."

"The Order makes exceptions for those that are

great threats."

"No," Caydn said firmly. "I do not feel such measures are necessary in this situation."

The others nodded to Caydn in polite acknowledgement. It was then that Kieran noticed the glint of a metallic pendant on Caydn's chest.

A captain's crest, Kieran thought. *No wonder they listened to him.*

Suddenly, dread overtook Kieran.

I just attacked a Captain of the Flamemaster's Guard, he realized grimly. *Now I've really had it!*

Kieran sank down onto the floor of the cell as the other members of the guard departed once more. Caydn, however, stayed firmly planted by the door. Finally, he spoke.

"You've stirred up a great deal of trouble, youngling."

Kieran stayed quiet. His mouth typically got him into trouble and he really couldn't afford any more of that at the moment.

Caydn watched him curiously before turning away from the cell once more. Kieran breathed a sigh of relief. He looked down and noticed that his hands were shaking and his head was throbbing.

What is going on? Kieran pondered worriedly.

A new voice called out. "You have overexerted, young mage."

Kieran jumped. The voice had a lighter tone than Caydn's deep rumble. He nervously looked around the cell but no one was present.

"Where are you?" Kieran called out softly. He watched to make sure Caydn hadn't taken notice.

"You do not have to call out to me."

Kieran was puzzled. "I don't understand," he whispered.

With an abrupt jolt, Kieran felt a surge in the magic that flowed through his body. As if it moved on its own, Kieran's hand raised and a small feather-like flame hovered above his palm. He watched in amazement as it flickered before quickly dissipating as the last had done.

You're my magic! Kieran thought excitedly. *But how can I hear you?*

"All in good time, young mage," the voice said softly. "You need rest."

At least tell me your name, Kieran implored.

The voice rippled through his mind. "I am Akiri."

Chapter Two
The High Seat and the Representative

Kieran awoke groggily the next morning to the sound of a metal tray being slid into his cell. By the time he could open his eyes, the iron door had already been shut and locked. Kieran scrambled over to find a bowl filled with fruit and oatmeal.

Kieran's stomach growled, and he hastily grabbed a spoon from the tray. He scarfed down several bites barely noticing the taste. Although it satisfied his hunger, Kieran realized there was hardly any flavor to the fruit in the bowl. He shrugged it off and continued to dig in. Bland food was better than no food.

Kieran spent the rest of the morning in agonizing silence. Except for the echoing footsteps of the passing guards, there was no sound. He was used to the busy street noise of Tarmuth. As the capital city of Peria, Tarmuth was home to a bustling population. Kieran longed to hear the trundle of carts, the calls of market vendors, and even the shooing of a shopkeeper urging him along.

Any sound at all would be better than this.

The absence of sunlight left Kieran feeling disoriented. The Moonstone glowed ever constant, and the oatmeal had been the only real sign of morning. No birds could be heard singing through the thick stone walls or any other sound that would denote the time of day.

He laid his head back against the smooth stone wall at what he guessed to be midday. His mind was whirling with questions.

Akiri? He hoped his thought would reach the strange presence. There was only silence for a moment, but then Kieran felt a stirring.

"Yes?" came the smooth tones of Akiri.

Kieran's thoughts felt jumbled now, and he didn't know how to sort them out. He hadn't thought through what to do if Akiri responded.

How can I talk to you? Kieran asked bravely. *I always thought magic was just an unseen force.*

"Magic is many things," Akiri answered. "It ebbs and flows just like the passing of time."

Can everyone speak with their magic? Kieran asked.

"No," came Akiri's reply. "It is not a common occurrence in your time."

Kieran wondered what Akiri meant by that, but before he could ask, he noticed Caydn approaching his cell. He tensed, unsure of why such a high-ranking Flamemaster would be returning.

"How are you, young mage?" Caydn's deep voice inquired.

"Wonderful," Kieran replied sarcastically. "I've rather enjoyed this place."

"I was more concerned with how you are feeling," Caydn replied, sounding less than amused with Kieran's attitude. "A magical feat such as the one you attempted last night is very strenuous to an untrained mage."

And why do you care? Kieran thought bitterly, but he knew well enough to keep quiet.

"He seems different," came the mysterious voice of Akiri.

He probably wants something, Kieran thought warily.

Caydn stood sternly on the other side of the iron bars. Kieran glared defiantly at him, remaining silent as stone.

Finally, Caydn spoke.

"Tomorrow you will go before the Keepers of the Order. They will determine what path you shall find yourself on since this... incident. I would strongly encourage you to hold your tongue in check when addressing the Keepers, especially High Seat Elrayan. Show respect, stay calm, and speak only when spoken to."

"Why are you telling me this?" Kieran asked suspiciously.

Caydn paused. He looked directly at Kieran.

"I feel the Order owes everyone a fair chance, no matter their transgressions," he replied. "Your path diverges in front of you, young mage. You ultimately decide which route you will take. Choose wisely."

With that, Caydn turned and disappeared into the darkness, leaving Kieran confused and frustrated.

Elves! Kieran exclaimed, frustrated with Caydn's cryptic message. Most Sombrayns were more plain-spoken and typically left the mysterious wisdom to their Veshtu cousins. However, Kieran assumed Caydn's demeanor was typical of a high-ranking member of the Order.

Kieran wrestled with the meaning behind Caydn's words for the rest of the afternoon. Eventually, another Sombrayn brought his dinner tray. He stayed still while the guard cautiously opened the door just enough to slide the tray inside.

Kieran found a bowl of warm broth, a piece of tough bread, and a small portion of roasted chicken. It was bland, just as breakfast had been, but he was grateful for something to fill his belly.

As he settled onto the bare mattress for the second night, his mind raced with the possibilities of the day ahead. He had heard tales of the rulings of the Keepers all his life. While most typical townsfolk had no cause to fear the Keepers of the Order, Kieran found himself in a slightly different position.

Without a family to raise Kieran in the ways of the Order, he curtailed the rules slightly to survive life on the streets. He had learned to be resourceful when it came to meeting certain needs; for clothing, he would clean the shop of a tailor for a new tunic or a pair of breeches. Food was easy enough to come by; he helped several widows in exchange for meals. However, the needs of a young mage are unique, especially one without training.

As a human, Kieran should have had less magical ability than most. However, that wasn't the case. From an early age, he had always felt the draw towards magic, particularly the conjuring of fire. He had always enjoyed watching the Sombrayns lighting the torches, and before long he had taught himself how to draw heat from the flames to keep warm. That sort of untaught magic was opposite of the ways of the Order.

The Order believed a mage should be in full control of their magic and that was achieved only through careful instruction and training. Self-taught mages were seen as a threat to the careful community the Order had worked hard to maintain.

"Do not fear what lies ahead," Akiri said unexpectantly to Kieran, jolting him from his though

That's easy for you to say, he replied, still getting used to hearing a voice inside his head. *You're not the one facing the Keepers.*

"I am with you," Akiri assured him. "You will not face this challenge alone."

Kieran tried to take comfort in Akiri's words, but worries still flooded his mind. Finally, he quietened his thoughts long enough to fall into a restless sleep.

*   *   *   *   *   *

Morning brought another bowl of bland oatmeal. Kieran ate quickly, not knowing when he would be retrieved and brought before the Keepers.

It wasn't long before several members of the fire guard arrived to transport Kieran to the meeting chambers. They sternly collected him from his cell, bound his hands, and set off towards the center of the city.

Kieran shut his eyes a moment as they entered the

streets. The sun's rays blinded him momentarily, but it was comforting to be back in the open. For a moment, his nerves calmed, and he happily took in the sights and sounds around him.

People of every race filled the crowded streets. Humans, elven-kind, centaurs, and canine-like Lycalians interacted cheerfully with each other. Some people stopped to stare curiously at Kieran and the fire guard as they passed.

Any time Kieran got distracted and slowed his pace, one of the guards would firmly urge him on. The disciplined steps of the guards echoed off the cobblestone. He counted the cadence in his head.

One, two. One, two. One, two.

They walked for so long that Kieran's feet began to ache. At last they reached a large building. Tall wooden doors stood at its entrance and regal Lycalian soldiers flanked each side.

Kieran looked into the Lycalians' furry faces. Their fur was gray and coarse. Atop their canine heads were shiny metal helmets. They wore lightweight leather armor and bore no visible weapons. Kieran knew it was because of their proficiency with the earth artes. Suddenly he felt uneasy, fully aware that either of these Lycalian soldiers could cause the very ground to spring up around him.

One of the Lycalians stepped aside as they approached and opened the massive door. Kieran was led inside.

He was taken aback by the beauty of the room. It

had to have been constructed by elven builders. No other race put such delicate curls and embellishments in their architecture.

The ceiling seemed to stretch upward forever. Large, open archways lined the walls, letting in rays of golden sunlight.

The guards led Kieran through the entry into a smaller holding room. Half of the fire guard now departed from Kieran and made their way through an open doorway into the main council chamber. Kieran could hear the chatter and see the movement of those gathering in the room ahead.

The waiting seemed endless to Kieran, and he started to feel very nervous. However, Caydn's words echoed in his head. *Show respect. Stay calm. Speak only when spoken to.*

Kieran repeated the words over and over again. As he started to calm down, a tall, silvery-haired elven man entered the room. Unlike the short-haired Sombrayn elves, this one's hair was long and flowed past his shoulders. His skin was olive and his eyes were a bright, vivid blue. He wore an aqua blue silk tunic that buttoned up to his chin. Delicate designs were emblazoned throughout the garment in thin silver thread.

He's Veshtu, Kieran thought. Veshtu elves were very regal and composed, unlike their bold Sombrayn counterparts. Whereas Sombrayn elves excelled at flame magic, a Veshtu's power lied in the softer artes: water wielding and healing magic.

"Bring him forth," the Veshtu elf commanded.

His voice was soft and light, like morning dew on grass.

The guards prodded Kieran forward. His feet moved on their own; his nerves couldn't have carried him an inch. The noise of those gathered grew ever louder as Kieran stepped into the main council chamber.

If the entry room had been grand, this one was exquisite. As with the other, large open archways invited the surrounding nature inside. Though the building sat in the heart of the city, ornate gardens encircled it on all sides. Flowers of every color grew just outside the edges of the room. Their fragrant smell wafted inside.

An array of brightly colored birds chirped and flew in and out of the room. Some looked more like streaks of light than actual living creatures. Such was typical of much of Peria's magical wildlife. Creatures of all shapes and sizes were a part of the magical cycle of life just as much as any of the sentient races.

Deerlings, magical deer-like creatures, grazed contentedly just out of reach. They didn't seem bothered by the buzzing crowd. Kieran's gaze fell on a particularly small one. Its body shimmered in the light like sun sparkling on a lake. This one had a faintly orange hue. It raised its head and caught Kieran's gaze. He could sense the flow of flame magic coursing through the little deerling. The creature watched Kieran briefly before turning back to eat the sweet grass.

Kieran had been so focused on the deerling that he had neglected his surroundings. The fire guard had led him to the exact center of the meeting chamber. Carved wooden benches curved around much of the room. They were quickly filling with occupants.

An ornate podium stood unoccupied at the head of the room. Kieran assumed it was meant for High Seat Elrayan.

A hush fell as eight men and women filed into the room. They found seats at two long tables on either side of the podium.

The Keepers of the Order, Kieran thought to himself. The eight were all in formal silver robes with no identifying embellishments. Elven, human, and Lycalian faces stared silently at Kieran.

An attendant entered the room behind the eight and cleared his throat. He motioned for everyone to rise. With all in attendance up on their feet, Elrayan at last stepped into the room.

Elrayan wore long silken robes of crystal blue, adorned even more lavishly than the Veshtu tunic Kieran had seen earlier. Embroidered patterns of birds and flora graced the entire garment. Elrayan's hair was a golden hue and fell neatly between his shoulder blades. His Alderan heritage was apparent; they were the most physically and magically diverse of the three elven races.

"Greetings, friends of the Order," Elrayan addressed the crowd. "Please find your seats so we may begin with today's proceedings."

Kieran had known Elrayan only in name before today and was puzzled by this man's disposition. For the face of the Keepers of the Order, he seemed rather warm and inviting.

That feeling quickly faded once the formalities

were finished. Elrayan turned a cold, glaring eye to Kieran.

"Young man, it seems you've caused the city of Tarmuth a great deal of trouble. The damage done to the Hall of Founders might be irreparable."

Caydn's warning echoed again in Kieran's head. He wanted to declare his innocence, but knew it would be best to hold his tongue.

Kieran's thoughts trailed off as he scanned the crowd. His gaze fell upon the aforementioned elf. Kieran recognized the smooth crescent scar on Caydn's cheek. Caydn's face was turned as he talked to another Sombrayn elf to his right. This man stared directly at Kieran as Caydn whispered unknown words in his ear. This elf was even taller than most and broad, even in Sombrayn terms. His dark hair was wild and a thin, singular long braid hung across his left shoulder.

"The accused shall answer!" Elrayan admonished, startling Kieran. He had been too distracted to hear Elrayan's question.

"Does the accused have representation?" Elrayan repeated in a frustrated tone.

"Um…" Kieran stammered.

"The accused does indeed have representation," a voice called from the crowd.

Heads turned in the voice's direction. It had come from the strange Sombrayn beside Caydn, who rose to his feet and made his way to the center of the room.

"Ah, Master Hartlan," High Seat Elrayan said, not sounding a bit surprised. "Have you come to represent the accused?"

"Yes, as it should be noted," Hartlan replied formally. He cast a cheeky glance at Kieran and gave him a wink. He then turned back to Elrayan.

"Well, shall we get started?"

Chapter Three
The Order's Ruling

Kieran didn't know what to think of the new Sombrayn. Master Hartlan, as High Seat Elrayan had called him, had risen from the crowd and came to stand at Kieran's side.

Kieran looked up at the elf towering over him. He wore a plain, gray travel robe. The reaction of the crowd made Kieran think he must be someone of importance.

Who is this man?

It took a few moments for the room to settle back into order. Elrayan addressed Master Hartlan.

"The Keepers of the Order recognize Master Hartlan as representative for the accused," Elrayan said with importance. "Now, the witnesses to the event of two days' past shall come forward to present their testimony."

Kieran listened as witness after witness came forward, each with a different account of what had happened. All spoke of the flames that had raged out of control, but none seemed to know how they had actually started.

Akiri? Kieran's thoughts strayed from those speaking. *Did you start the fire in the streets?*

"No," came Akiri's calm voice.

Though Kieran still knew little about this new

voice, he felt that Akiri had answered truthfully.

Then what do you believe happened? Kieran asked. *And why does everyone think it was me?*

"That I do not know."

As the witnesses continued their accounts, Kieran tried desperately to recall what had happened. Again, all he remembered was watching the torches being lit before his memory faltered.

As Elrayan dismissed the last witness, Kieran started to feel strange. His head began throbbing, and he found himself unable to reach out to Akiri.

Something felt dark and wild inside of Kieran, and he cried out. Guards rushed at him, but Hartlan quickly stepped between them. He pulled up his sleeve and placed his hand on Kieran's back.

"Breathe," Hartlan said firmly to Kieran.

Kieran's head pounded and his vision began to blur. He tried again in vain to speak to Akiri.

"Breathe, young mage!" Hartlan urged again. "Find your magic!"

"Guards, restrain this young man!" Elrayan called out, a mixture of fear and anger in his voice.

"No!" Hartlan protested. "You mustn't come near!" The guards stopped reluctantly and eyed him warily. Hartlan motioned for Caydn who quickly rushed to him.

"His initial talent lies in flame," Caydn said to Hartlan. "I've seen it."

Hartlan nodded and raised his hands. He rolled them in a circular motion. Flames emerged from his palms.

Kieran noticed the flash of flames, but couldn't move. He collapsed to the floor sweating and shaking.

"Come now, young mage," Hartlan urged. "You must stand!"

Kieran felt pairs of hands lift him to his feet. He couldn't see their faces, but they held him firmly. Hartlan stepped directly in front of him, still holding the flames.

"Now, reach out to the flame," Hartlan commanded.

I can't, Kieran thought, feeling weak and dizzy.

"Yes, you can," Akiri's voice soothed. Kieran felt relieved to hear him again.

Hartlan made the flames grow and Kieran reached toward them. The fire leapt from Hartlan to Kieran's outstretched hand. It twisted and swirled through the air. The warmth of the magic coursed through Kieran's body and he finally drew in a good, deep breath. His body no longer shook.

"Move the fire," Akiri encouraged. Kieran raised his arms, and the flames curled around them and down his body. Even though he could feel the heat, the magical fire did not burn Kieran's skin.

"Now it is time to dismiss it," Akiri said. Kieran felt the nudge, and he lowered his arms. The flames faded into embers and then seemed to disappear into thin air. Kieran felt tired, yet invigorated.

"Very good, young mage," Hartlan whispered.

Elrayan did not look so pleased. He raised his nose high in the air and cleared his throat.

"Guards! Subdue this Wilder!"

"This boy is not a Wilder!" Hartlan said boldly to Elrayan. "To label him as such is ridiculous and unfounded!"

"Only a Wilder would exhibit such a lack of control in the presence of the Order!" Elrayan spat angrily.

"The boy may lack control," Hartlan began. "However, you know even better than I that a true Wilder would not be so easily subdued."

"Be that as it may," Elrayan sneered. "This boy still stands accused…"

"He stands accused of a crime that he could not have committed," Hartlan interrupted. "The fires that consumed the streets and the Hall of the Founders were unfortunate, but of a far greater ability than this young mage is capable of. Perhaps it was the work of a Wilder, though you will find no Wilder here before you today!"

Hartlan continued as he walked toward the crowd. "Someone is responsible for the destruction caused, that is true. I have every confidence that the Keepers of the Order will continue to be diligent in their efforts to uncover the truth."

Hartlan turned back to Kieran. "Just as the Keepers have their duties to uphold, so do I. I see this young mage in need of training and extend the offer to attend the Academy of Magic."

Murmurs rippled through the crowd. Elrayan waved his hands slowly to quieten the chatter.

"While your offer is genuinely appreciated, the

Keepers of the Order will need time to confer and come to a decision regarding this matter."

Elrayan turned to the other eight Keepers. They spoke in hushed voices to one another. Finally, an elven woman arose.

"Master Hartlan, the Keepers of the Order recognize your prowess as leader of the Academy of Magic and commends your dedication to the young mages of Peria. We find your offer acceptable on one condition."

After a short pause, she continued. "The boy will be released into the care of the Academy under the condition that you will stand accountable for any of his forthcoming actions."

"I accept," Hartlan said with a nod of his head.

"Then the Keepers of the Order declare that the charges brought against this young man be dropped so long as he agrees to undergo magical training."

All eyes were on Kieran. He tried to wrap his head around the flurry of words.

"I agree," Kieran replied tentatively.

The woman spoke once more. "Then the Keepers of the Order thank all in attendance. You are dismissed."

The crowd collectively rose to their feet and began to exit the room. Kieran was left standing in the middle, flabbergasted.

Hartlan approached Kieran once more. "We'd best be off," he said, letting out a sigh of relief. "It is a day's journey to the Academy."

Hartlan escorted Kieran to the far side of the

room. Caydn gave Kieran a small nod of the head as they passed. As they reached the doorway, Kieran looked back one last time.

He locked eyes with Elrayan who looked shocked by the outcome of events. Something about the look in Elrayan's eyes made Kieran feel uneasy. He quickly turned back around and followed closely on Master Hartlan's heels.

Chapter Four
Horses and Honeycakes

Kieran had to run to keep up with Hartlan's long stride. He followed the Academy leader back out of the meeting chamber and into the bustling streets of Tarmuth. As they strolled through the city in silence, Kieran's excitement grew.

The Academy of Magic was well-renowned in Peria. There was no better place to learn the magical artes. Kieran had never expected to have a chance to go.

"Have you ever been outside of Tarmuth?" Hartlan asked, glancing back at Kieran.

"No," Kieran replied, jogging to keep up. "I've lived here my whole life."

It was a bit intimidating to fathom that he was about to leave his lifelong home. However, the prospect of seeing new places was something Kieran had always dreamed of.

"How will we get to the Academy?" Kieran asked.

"Typically mages travel by blinkpoints though it takes some training to learn how to do so," Hartlan explained. "So I have arranged us a carriage. We are on our way to meet it."

Onward they made their way through the city. As

Kieran passed by familiar places and people, he felt a twinge of sadness. The feeling quickly faded as Kieran caught sight of a massive purple carriage up ahead. A team of golden horses was hitched to the front. Their manes were braided, as were their tails. They tossed their heads and whinnied as Hartlan and Kieran drew near.

As they reached the carriage, a small Lycalian man popped out from inside it. Most of the Lycalians Kieran had seen were tall and broad. This man, however, was far shorter than Kieran and very slender. His gray, furry ears were erect and his mouth was parted in an excited smile.

"Master Hartlan," the Lycalian's voice came out in an excited, high-pitched squeak. "Are you ready for departure?"

"We are," Hartlan gestured to Kieran.

"Is this a new student?" the Lycalian asked excitedly.

"He is. This is Kieran."

"Very nice to meet you, young master!" the Lycalian bounced forward and grabbed Kieran's hand. He shook it vigorously. "I am Pip."

"Nice to meet you, Pip," Kieran replied.

Pip turned his attention to Hartlan. "Master Hartlan, there are treats prepared for you and the young master inside the carriage."

"My greatest thanks," Hartlan said kindly. He turned to Kieran. "We are ready to depart."

Kieran climbed up into the carriage. He lightly touched some golden leaves decorating the outside before stepping into the interior. Plush seat cushions were upholstered in a matching bright, golden fabric. The shade closely matched the horses' coats. Rich, plum colored curtains hung across the small windows. Beneath one window sat a dark, wooden shelf laden with cakes and pastries of all sorts. Kieran's stomach growled hungrily at the sight.

Hartlan climbed in after Kieran and saw him eyeing the cakes. He grabbed a fruit pastry and took a large bite.

"Delicious!" Hartlan said warmly. "Please, help yourself."

Kieran grabbed a sticky honey cake. He took a small bite and quickly followed it up with another as sweet honey filled his mouth. Kieran had never tasted anything so decadent.

As he ate, Kieran heard Pip call out to the horses, and the carriage lurched forward. Kieran settled back onto the gold cushions and grabbed another cake. He watched Hartlan reach down below the shelf and pull up a silver pitcher and two goblets. Steam rose into the air as he poured a liquid into the goblet and passed it to Kieran.

"Warm apple cider," Hartlan stated as Kieran took the cup. He took a sip as Hartlan pulled open the curtains. Kieran peered out in time to see the carriage clearing the city gates.

Kieran drank in the varying sites as they rode through the countryside. It was all so green! Kieran had mainly known only cobblestone beneath his feet.

Open fields stretched before them with mountains

and forests in the distance. The road seemed rather straight for a good deal of time. Eventually, he became less interested in the sights and started thinking again.

What a crazy past few days!

He looked at Hartlan who had his head reclined against the back of the seat, eyes closed. *What a strange man!* Kieran thought.

He had so many questions still buzzing in his head. Finally, his curiosity overcame him.

"Master Hartlan?" Kieran asked. Hartlan immediately opened his eyes.

"Yes, Kieran?"

"I wanted to thank you for everything you've done for me. I really owe you my neck. But…" Kieran paused. "I just don't understand why you did it."

"I assume that though you've heard of the Academy, you know very little about it, correct?" Hartlan asked.

"Right," Kieran answered.

"Then perhaps it will help if I explain the mission of the Academy."

"It sure would," Kieran said, not intending to sound rude, but realizing that it might have been.

Hartlan didn't seem to take offense. "The Academy of Magic has existed for centuries to help train young mages with their magical gifts. Now, most of the more innate magical races: elves, Lycalians, centaurs, among others, teach their own children while they are young. This is not always so, mind you. There are many who are not so fortunate. Also, with the sporadic nature of human magic, often a parent will have a different ability than their child and will be unable to teach them properly. Thus, the need for a central place of training arose."

"The Mages of the early Order felt it would be best to establish a place for these young mages to go where all could have access to the training they needed. Hence, the Academy of Magic was born. The Academy has carried the task of training mages ever since."

Kieran soaked in Hartlan's words. It all sounded great, but Kieran still had many questions. He knew that hearing the voice of his magic was not normal, but he hesitated to ask Hartlan about it.

Doubts of Akiri's intentions began to form in Kieran's mind. He wondered why he had never heard the voice of his magic before now.

"It should be noted that mages vary greatly in ability in the early stages of their training." Hartlan's voice shook Kieran from his thoughts. "You were called a name by the High Seat during your hearing. Do you recall what it was?"

"He called me a Wilder."

"And do you know what that means?"

"Not exactly," Kieran said. "I know that Wilders go against the teachings of the Order."

"A Wilder," Hartlan explained, "is a mage whose magic has become the master. The mage can no longer control his or her own power. The magic acts of its own volition."

Kieran was silent. Akiri seemed to act of his own will.

Hartlan watched Kieran expectantly, but Kieran stayed quiet.

Maybe this is a good thing, Kieran thought to

himself. *If I go to the Academy, I can learn to control Akiri, and then no one will have to know.*

They rode on in silence for several hours. The sky became streaked in the majestic reds and oranges of sunset. It was then that Kieran noticed the carriage was no longer on the main road. He looked out the window and couldn't see any nearby cities or villages.

Pip slowed the horses to a stop. The carriage bumped as the wheels halted. Kieran was quick to poke his head outside.

Pip swiftly hopped down from the driver's position carrying a bundle.

"If you'd be so kind, young master, I could use some help pitching the tent," Pip chirped.

Kieran nodded and followed Pip. They started unfolding the cloth and raising the stakes. After several moments of awkward fumbling, a crooked tent stood before them.

Hartlan came up beside them and began raising his own tent. Pip rushed off to start a fire and gather some rations from a storage compartment in the carriage. He came back carrying a bucket.

"Young master," Pip waved the bucket about. "There's a stream not far past that tree." He pointed to a small, scraggly tree. "If you would fetch us some water, I'll have some stew prepared once you return."

Kieran took the bucket and started off toward the stream. He was suddenly acutely aware that he was in *very* odd company. Hartlan surely had plenty of his own mysteries, and Pip? Well, Pip was certainly strange.

Kieran started to hear the gentle sound of moving

water. In the twilight it was difficult to make out the footpath, and he tripped over a rock. The bucket flew out of Kieran's hand as he landed flat on his stomach.

"Ow!"

Kieran yelled out in frustration. He suddenly felt the heat of his magic welling inside of him. The familiar feeling brought his thoughts back to the night in the streets of Tarmuth. Kieran could remember feeling that same surge before he had been caught by the fire guard.

The rest of his memory was still clouded. Kieran began to feel fearful that Akiri was keeping something from him. He tried to repress the magic rising in his chest.

Kieran had little success. Waves of energy coursed through his body, but he could not gain control of it. Finally, as it started to overpower Kieran, Akiri's voice rang out.

"Remember the flames from this morning," Akiri said firmly. "Raise your arms. Call the flame forth and direct it!"

Kieran obeyed, and to his surprise, bright flickering flames shot from his hands. He raised his arms like Akiri said, and the fire danced around his body.

Kieran was bewildered. *I've done it! I've wielded on my own!* He thought excitedly.

"Good," Akiri said. "Now, remember. Lower your arms to dismiss the flame."

Kieran ignored Akiri's instructions. He moved his arms slowly through the air and watched in amazement as the fire bent to his command. He was feeling giddy from the power and didn't notice his legs shaking.

"I don't want to dismiss it!" Kieran called out

excitedly, emboldened by the power he felt.

"No," Akiri said firmly. "It's too much. You cannot maintain it. Dismiss it!"

Kieran refused to relent. Suddenly, his body gave out, and he fell forward. The last thing he heard was Akiri calling out his name and the faint sound of water.

Chapter Five
Journeying On

"Kieran? Kieran!"

Kieran opened his eyes and found Master Hartlan standing over him.

"What happened?" Kieran asked, finding it hard to recall.

"That's the same question I had for you," Master Hartlan said, mild concern in his voice. Hartlan extended his hand to Kieran and pulled him to a sitting position.

"I... I must have tripped and hit my head," Kieran lied, thinking it best not to tell Hartlan of the voice he was hearing. "I don't really remember."

Kieran tried to determine if Master Hartlan had bought the lie or not. Hartlan's face was stoic; Kieran couldn't tell.

"Darkness is falling," Hartlan said. "We'd best return for the night." He helped Kieran to his feet, and they headed back toward the camp.

Pip greeted them each with a bowl of stew. Kieran ate a few bites, but after what had just happened, he really didn't have much of an appetite. Kieran thanked Pip for the stew, declined a second portion, and crawled inside the little, lopsided tent.

Kieran lay there replaying the events of the

evening over and over in his head. He should have felt happier; he had just produced a flame by himself. However, a nagging feeling began to stir inside Kieran.

Why did you stop me? Kieran tried to ask Akiri, but the mysterious presence gave no response. Frustration welled inside of Kieran. He rolled to his side and closed his eyes, eventually drifting to sleep.

*   *   *   *   *   *

Morning brought birdsong and a big pot of porridge. Kieran, still grappling with his feelings toward Akiri, quickly ate a small bowl before rising to his feet.

"Thank you, Pip," Kieran said, handing his bowl back to the Lycalian. Pip offered Kieran another portion.

"I'm going for a walk," Kieran said, politely declining.

"We will depart shortly," Hartlan said, emerging from his large tent.

"I won't be long," Kieran assured him. "I just want to stretch my legs before we leave."

Kieran hurried back down the footpath towards the stream. Once he felt he was safely out of sight, he slowed his pace. He eventually reached the same spot from the night before. Closing his eyes, Kieran took in slow even breaths. He raised his arms, trying to draw out the warm energy pulsing in his chest and…

Nothing.

Confused, Kieran tried again. He thought back to how Hartlan had summoned the flames in the Keepers' chambers. He held his arms out and twisted his wrists in a circular motion.

Still nothing.

Why can't I wield? Kieran asked angrily.

"Let me help you," Akiri offered.

No! Kieran snapped. *I can do it on my own. I don't need your help!* He tried again and again, but still could not conjure a flame. Finally, he let out a frustrated yell and gave up.

Kieran paused before returning to the camp to splash his face with the frigid water of the stream. The icy droplets stung his freckled skin, but the cold shock helped quell the rising anger he felt inside. He rose from the stream and made his way back to the camp.

Hartlan and Pip had already dismantled the tents and had the carriage reloaded. The horses pawed the ground anticipating the coming journey. Kieran walked past Hartlan and Pip without a word and climbed inside the carriage, still sulking.

Hartlan joined Kieran. Pip let out a loud call to the horses, and they took off. Kieran's bad mood continued as they set off once more.

"We shall reach the Academy by mid-afternoon," Hartlan said.

"Great," Kieran said flatly, his arms crossed over his chest.

"Once we arrive, you'll be assigned a student guide, one who has been with the Academy for some time now. They will help see that you settle in and…"

"Wonderful," Kieran interrupted with a sarcastic bite.

Hartlan paused, looking over the moody twelve-year-old. "I know this must be difficult, Kieran," Hartlan began. "Leaving the only home you've ever known..."

"I'm glad you know what I'm feeling," Kieran snapped. "You seem to know everything."

Kieran regretted the words as soon as he said them. He braced himself for Hartlan's retaliation, but Hartlan just looked rather amused.

"I'm sorry," Kieran said sheepishly. "I didn't mean..."

"No need to apologize." Hartlan's voice was steady and calm.

"I don't know what's happening to me," Kieran stammered. "I feel so... so... *different* lately."

Hartlan seemed to think for a moment.

"We live in a world of the Order," he said at last. "From a very young age, we are told what is right and how we are to connect with the magic that flows within us."

"For the most part, I agree," Hartlan continued. "We do need to be aware of the power we all hold inside us. However, one thing the Order does not take into account is how different each person can be."

"The magic that flows through the land of Peria is deeply connected. Think of it as you would a spider's web. On and on it spins and connections travel further and further. Your magic, I suspect, is deeply at the center of this magical web. It's the reason you can reach out and touch another mage's magic, as you did with mine yesterday. Your magic thrives on the connections you form with others."

"But isn't that bad?" Kieran asked. "To connect to another mage's magic?"

"It doesn't have to be," Hartlan explained. "Magic is deeply complex, just as those who wield it."

"But Elrayan said..."

"Elrayan and others like him often see only small portions of the true intentions of the Order," Hartlan cut in. "The Order began to strengthen the magical community. Throughout history, however, it has ebbed and changed. Things that were once understood and accepted are not always as prevalent."

"The Order of today's age has grown wary. They feel it is best if all mages learn to control their magic the same way. I believe differently. I believe we are no longer in the age of the Order."

Hartlan grew quiet allowing Kieran some time to think. However, he didn't have long before a breathtaking sight came into view. The fields and forests of their journey gave way to the sight of a large, sparkling lake. Past the lake laid a great, sweeping hill, and perched at the top was a magnificent castle. Banners of bold colors danced in the wind. Scattered around the base of the hill were a slew of small buildings and structures. Kieran leaned out the window to take it all in.

The carriage trundled on past the lake and up the hill. Pip let out a "Whoa!" and slowed the horses just before the castle gate. He opened the door enthusiastically for Kieran. Kieran stepped down from the carriage before the castle.

Hartlan smiled. "Welcome to the Academy of Magic."

Chapter Six
Arrival at the Gates

Kieran gazed up in amazement at the massive stone castle. The impressive structure made Kieran feel both small and somehow big at the same time. Something about its stony face felt more welcoming than imposing.

A crowd of young faces gathered around Kieran and Hartlan. Humans, elves, Lycalians, and centaurs all gawked excitedly at Kieran.

"A new student!" Kieran heard them whisper.

"Looks human!" said another. Her voice held excitement, not disdain.

Several students approached Hartlan and spoke with him. They seemed perfectly comfortable to address him informally. Hartlan had dropped the formalities he had held before the Keepers of the Order and spoke to the students warmly. After a few moments, Hartlan brought two fingers to his lips and let out a whistle. A hush immediately fell over the crowd.

"Greetings, dear students and teachers!" Hartlan's voice echoed off the stone. "I am glad to find you all well on this fine day! I'm sure most of you are curious of my recent absence. My friends, I have found another young mage ready to join our esteemed Academy!"

Master Hartlan nudged Kieran forward. "This, my

dear students, is Kieran of Tarmuth!"

The crowd greeted Kieran warmly. Several stepped up to shake his hand or pat him on the back.

"Now," Hartlan continued. "I know we've just experienced a good deal of excitement; however, you all have studies to attend to, and I'm sure our young friend is eager to get settled in."

A couple of disappointed groans came from the crowd. Nevertheless, they started to leave all except for a Veshtu girl about Kieran's age. She made her way to the front of the throng, her silvery-blonde hair billowing behind her.

"Master Hartlan," she began, her voice crisp. "May I speak with you?"

"Of course, Luri!" Master Hartlan replied charismatically. "I had also intended to speak with you. Follow me."

Hartlan started off, then turned to speak to Kieran.

"Pip will give you a tour of the grounds. Dinner is served at dusk in the dining hall. Get your rest tonight, for you will have your evaluation test tomorrow."

"Test? What test?" Kieran called after him, but Master Hartlan was already too far away to hear him. Pip bustled up and tugged at Kieran's sleeve.

"Ready, young master?"

Kieran nodded. Pip turned on his heels and Kieran dashed after him. For such a short little Lycalian, Pip definitely was fast!

Pip lead Kieran away from the castle back down the hill toward the buildings below.

"The Academy has grown to its students' needs throughout the centuries," Pip explained. "The main castle holds most of the common areas: the dining hall, library, recovery wing, classrooms, and is home to some of the students, particularly most elven kind and humans."

"Now, the rest of the grounds provide housing to the students better suited to open spaces, such as Lycalians, centaurs, and Reshmayans."

Students made their way in and out of small wooden lodgings only big enough for one or two. Sitting on top of one of the little houses was a spectacled Lycalian boy reading a rather thick book. Pip called out to him. It startled the Lycalian at first, then he seemed to recognize Pip. He looked down and waved.

"My nephew, Pembran," Pip explained.

Pembran slid down from the roof and landed nimbly in front of Kieran and Pip. He was nearly twice as tall as his uncle, though with the same charcoal gray fur. His ears were longer than Pip's and did not stand up on their own. Pembran pushed his glasses back up his furry snout.

"Have the horses been tended to?" Pembran asked Pip.

"They're being looked after, but you're welcome to assist!" Pip replied cheerfully. Pembran gave a nod and took off in a run toward the stables. Pip chuckled at Kieran's puzzled expression.

"Pembran is very fond of creatures of all sorts," Pip explained. "Sometimes his excitement gets a little carried away."

They continued on and Kieran drank in all the various sights and sounds. The bustle reminded him of Tarmuth. Groups of students scurried to and from the castle. Some carried books, whereas others were empty-handed. Flashes of magic all around startled Kieran at first, but to the other students it seemed completely normal to wield out in the open.

Kieran watched as an older Sombrayn student conjured a long, serpent-like flame. It writhed through the air carefully encircling several others. They barely took notice of its presence. Then a Veshtu elf stepped forward. He pulled his hands through the air above a small well. Delicate streams of water rose up and flowed through the air toward the flames. The Sombrayn smirked and raced his flame toward the water. The two magical manifestations collided, sending steam up into the air. The students let out happy laughter before continuing on their way.

It was so curious to Kieran. Never had he seen a display like that made in the open in Tarmuth. The Order forbade public displays of magic intended for entertainment. Magic was to be used for practical purposes: filling vessels with water, cooking, constructing buildings, and so forth.

Kieran reached out and grabbed Pip by the arm. He glanced back at the students. "This place is amazing, and I'm thankful to not be sitting in a cell, but I still have so many questions."

"As you should, young master!" Pip grinned.

Kieran expected him to say more, but the little Lycalian bounded back up the hill to the castle. Kieran sighed and raced after him.

As they reached the entrance gate, Kieran spotted Master Hartlan and the same Veshtu girl from before.

Luri, Kieran remembered. He looked up at her. She was at least a head taller than him and very slim. Thin strands of her long, gossamer hair were pulled from the sides and secured in the back. She looked at Kieran with a bit of a scowl.

"Ah, perfect timing!" Master Hartlan exclaimed. "The Academy can be very overwhelming to a new student. Kieran, meet your guide, Luri."

"Nice to meet you," Kieran said politely, holding out his hand.

Luri just nodded her head curtly. She looked disdainfully at his outstretched hand.

"That is more of a human custom," Luri said briskly.

Kieran dropped his hand back to his side. *Well, she's different,* he thought.

"Follow me," Luri said. She turned on her heels and glided through the gate. Kieran stumbled after her. Inside the gate was a cobbled courtyard. Stone figures sat all around it. Kieran saw likenesses of what he assumed were famous mages from history. He wanted to explore, but Luri urged him onward. They crossed into the threshold of the castle itself.

The ceiling stretched high above them and the walls in the entrance hall were a dark, sleek wood.

Different colored banners decorated the length of the hallway in green, aqua, scarlet, gold, and silver.

"Those denote the different clans of the Academy," Luri said shortly. When Kieran looked confused, she sighed and explained.

"First, the green. That pennant belongs to Clan Terra. Students in Terra are gifted in the earth artes."

"What does that mean?" Kieran asked.

"The earth artes encompass all magic that affects the natural world around us, whether it be aiding the growth of plants or the moving of stone." Luri pointed next at the aqua banner. "Blue markings refer to Clan Aqua. Aquaians lean toward the water artes. Then there is Clan Ignis, recognized by scarlet. I assume that will be your affinity, from what I've heard."

"What do you mean?"

"Clan Ignis are fire wielders," Luri explained. "Master Hartlan tells me you have abilities with the fire artes."

"Now," Luri said, moving on. "The last two clans are more unique. Students with abilities in multiple areas usually fall into either Clan Sunfire or Clan Moonglow. Sunfires are the most diverse in ability and lean toward the power artes, such as fire and earth. They are depicted by gold. Very few mages become Sunfires."

"Last, is Clan Moonglow. Moonglows, like Sunfires, are usually gifted in multiple artes, but whereas Sunfires learn bolder magic, Moonglows go more the path of healing and water artes."

Luri pointed at a silver pendant on her tunic. "I

belong to Clan Moonglow."

They had reached the end of the hallway and stood before a large oak door. Luri opened it effortlessly, and they stepped inside.

"The library," she announced, then motioned for Kieran to follow. They strode past shelf after shelf of books. Kieran had never seen so many books in his life, let alone in one room.

Along with the books were shelves filled with an array of other objects. Lenses, scales, bottles, just to name a few. There were even some objects Kieran could not identify, but before he had time to ask, Luri pushed him into a seat at a small wooden table.

She bounded off down an aisle of books, pulling one down, then another, adding to an ever growing pile in her arms.

Luri dropped the books loudly on the table in front of Kieran. She pulled one from the top of the stack.

"You should start with this one," she said hurriedly. "Master Kaya will expect you to know the initial wielding steps for the water artes."

"Who?" Kieran asked. He had no idea what Luri was talking about.

Luri closed her eyes and sighed sharply. "Master Kaya leads the water arte classes and is the head of Clan Aqua. She will be one of the teachers administering your evaluation test tomorrow."

"I don't know why I have to have an evaluation test," Kieran said testily. "I don't know any of the artes yet. Just put me in the beginner classes."

Luri rolled her eyes. "Your evaluation test doesn't just determine what classes you get placed in," she said haughtily. "First, and most importantly, it determines your Clan. Most mages start out in one of the three elemental Clans: Terra, Aqua, or Ignis. I started in Aqua. It is very rare for a mage to be placed in either Sunfire or Moonglow when they first come to the Academy. It took me six years to move to Clan Moonglow."

"Second," Luri continued. "The test will make sure that your magic is in accordance with the ways of the Order." She looked at Kieran with a serious expression. "We wouldn't want a Wilder joining the Academy."

Kieran swallowed. *What did Master Hartlan tell her about me?*

"She's very strict," a voice spoke up. *Akiri.*

Now isn't the best time, Akiri, Kieran thought sharply. *I need to focus.*

"You shouldn't worry," Akiri said. "I will help you tomorrow."

That's what I'm afraid of.

For the next couple of hours, Kieran and Luri poured over the gigantic stack of books. Luri droned on and on about the history of the Order, of the different teachers and classes, of the different forms for wielding, and dozens of other things. At last, the librarian, a thin Alderan elf, came by and urged the pair to head to dinner. Kieran bolted from his chair.

"Not yet," Luri scolded. "We need to study…"

"We need to eat," Kieran said firmly. "My head

48

already feels like it's going to explode!"

"Well, pardon me for trying to make sure you're prepared for tomorrow!" Luri's voice was high pitched.

"Listen," Kieran began. "I appreciate all the help, I really do, but I already know I'm going to be placed in Clan Ignis."

"Oh, really?" Luri said snidely. "And why do you believe that?"

"You said it earlier," Kieran answered. "Fire is the only arte I know. It's the only clan that would make sense."

Luri looked like she would argue. However, she shook her head. "Fine," she said. "If you feel prepared, then let's go to dinner."

*   *   *   *   *   *

The dinner table held more food than Kieran had ever seen in one place before. Roast chicken, meat pies, potatoes, greens, and plate after plate of more set at the head of the room. The students went up to it in droves, mounding food onto their plates. Kieran lost track of Luri and sidled up to the enormous table and began filling his plate.

Unsure of where to sit, Kieran found an empty table and made his way to it. He looked around and saw the colored pendants of the Clans pinned on everyone's tunics. Some wore clothing of their Clan color. They didn't separate into groups but instead mingled together.

Kieran noticed a large group of Ignis students sitting at a table to themselves. Most were Sombrayns, though there were a few humans and a Lycalian. One

Sombrayn kept staring at Kieran. He looked to be about the same age.

"That's Artemael," Luri whispered to Kieran. He jumped. He hadn't noticed her sit down beside him. "Artemael's brother, Master Kovesh, teaches the flame wielding classes. He's also the current head of Clan Ignis." She daintily picked up her fork and tucked into some roasted vegetables.

Kieran looked back at Artemael. He was still staring. Kieran held his gaze for a moment before Artemael turned back to his friends. Kieran went back to eating.

By the time his plate was licked clean, Kieran was so full he could hardly move. He groaned contentedly and rose slowly from the table. Luri stood with him.

"Master Hartlan has placed you in the room next to mine," she explained. "Come on, I will show you to your room."

They exited the dining room and made their way up a grand staircase. Kieran passed several more students that gave him curious glances.

Once they reached the top of the stairs, Luri led Kieran down a wide corridor.

"Welcome to the student quarters," Luri said. They walked to the far end of the corridor and turned down another hallway. About halfway down, Luri stopped.

"This is your room," she said, leading him inside. Kieran looked around at the modest bed and a small closet. On the bed was a pile of neatly folded shirts and pants. A note sat atop the pile. "For your new journey," it read. "Signed, Pip."

"It's not much," Luri said about the room, a slight pink color coming to her cheeks. "But it's comfortable. And if you need anything, my room is one further down the hall."

"Thanks," Kieran replied, still distracted by his surroundings.

Luri gave a soft wave and stepped out of the room, closing the door quietly behind her.

Kieran laid back on the bed and sank into the soft mattress. He closed his eyes. *What a day!* Kieran thought. The past few days, his entire world had changed. Kieran tried to imagine what the next day might bring, but the comfort of the bed lulled him to sleep.

Chapter Seven
The Journal

A gentle rapping on wood woke Kieran. He opened his eyes and called out.

"Just a minute!"

"Kieran?" came Luri's voice. "It's time to get up."

Kieran moaned and rolled out of the bed. Having a room of his own was still a new feeling to Kieran, and he longed to be back in bed from the moment he stood up.

He grabbed a blue tunic and a pair of tan pants from the stack at the end of the bed. He quickly got dressed, tried to smooth his unruly red hair, and then opened the door.

Luri stepped gracefully inside. Her pale hair was pulled up neatly into a smooth bun. She wore a silver shirt with burgundy embroidery. Her soft silver leather shoes carried her soundlessly across the floor. In her hand, she carried a slim journal and a quill.

"Good, you're already dressed." Luri opened the journal and crossed something out.

Kieran squinted at the quill. Luri didn't carry an ink well with her. She seemed to notice his confusion.

"Here at the Academy we use quills imbued with

runic magic," Luri stated matter-of-factly, holding the quill in the air. "It doesn't need ink."

"Well, that is... *functional*," Kieran said teasingly. Luri didn't seem to notice his tone. Her nose was buried in the journal. She looked up at Kieran, then back to her journal, then up again. Finally, she closed it.

"Is that really what you wish to wear?" she asked, staring at the blue tunic.

Kieran looked down at his chest. "I guess so. Why? Is something wrong with it?"

"Nothing is wrong with it," Luri said. "It's just... well, you want to make a good impression. If you go in wearing the Clan color you think you will be placed in, you will look more prepared."

"So I should wear red, right?"

"Well," Luri rambled breathlessly. "You don't want to appear cocky, so maybe you should wear a more neutral color."

Kieran scanned the pile. "I don't have anything neutral."

Luri put the tip of her quill to her lip. She tapped her foot for a moment, then brought it down suddenly.

"Ah, I know!" she said shrilly. "Wait here!"

Luri dashed out of the room leaving Kieran lost.

"She's very energetic," Akiri said.

That's one word for it, Kieran replied.

"I like her," Akiri stated.

Luri came bursting back into the room carrying a gray tunic. She thrust it at Kieran.

"Here," she said, panting a little. "It's my brother,

Shivyn's. Try it on."

"I don't really think they'll be judging what I'm wearing, Luri."

A spark came to Luri's eyes. "They will look at *everything*, Kieran!" Luri's voice was more high-pitched than usual.

"Okay, okay," Kieran said, putting his hands up. He grabbed the gray tunic. It had soft cream edging on it. Kieran thought it looked hideous. He looked at Luri who was staring intently at him.

"Do you mind?" he asked, motioning toward the door.

"Oh! Of course!" Luri stammered and stepped out into the hallway.

Kieran pulled off the blue shirt and slid the new gray one over his head. The material was thick and scratchy. It was even worse to wear than to look at. He went out into the hallway with Luri.

"Much better," she beamed. "You look very... distinguished."

Kieran couldn't tell if her pause had been because she was looking for the right word, or that she was trying to muster up some conviction.

"Your brother won't mind that I borrow his clothes?" Kieran asked.

Luri waved her hand. "Shivyn doesn't mind much of anything."

Kieran looked at Luri expectantly. She gave a little huff and looked back up from her journal. "Shivyn is very laid back. He's two years older than I am, and has been at the Academy longer, yet he has no ambition to move from Aqua to either Sunfire or Moonglow. He'd rather spend his time loafing around the castle or traipsing off to hike Mount Ulrah."

Kieran looked at Luri, who looked barely older than himself. He opened his mouth to ask, but immediately thought better of it. Luri seemed to read his mind.

"I'm fourteen," she said hastily.

"So that means you came to the Academy…"

"… when I was eight years old," Luri finished his sentence.

"Now," Luri said, opening her journal once more. "We have time for a short breakfast, then a meditation session…"

"Meditation?" Kieran asked, exasperated.

"Yes," Luri said firmly, snapping the journal closed again. "That way you can be mentally prepared." The journal flicked open again. "Then we will meet Cortyn for some light sparring, then…"

Kieran snatched the journal from Luri's fingers. He looked at the page and his jaw dropped as her checklist seemed to go on and on.

"Luri," Kieran said gently, handing the journal back. "I appreciate all the help, but I'm more of a 'wing-it' guy. It's just a test to place me. I'm not worried."

Luri took in another breath like she was having to stop herself from attacking Kieran. She breathed out slowly and her glowing eyes bore into his.

"First of all," she said through gritted teeth. "I've

already told you this is *not* just a test. This evaluation helps determine your entire future at the Academy. Second, Master Hartlan entrusted me to be your partner as you get acclimated here and I am not a 'wing-it' type of person at all."

"I just don't get it," Kieran argued. "If I get placed in the wrong Clan, can't I just move to another one later?"

"And lose years of useful training in the process? Absolutely not! Not under my watch!"

With that, Luri grabbed Kieran's wrist and dragged him to breakfast.

*   *   *   *   *   *

Kieran stared longingly at the pile of pastries that filled the long table at the head of the dining hall. Grumpily he shoveled some oatmeal into his mouth. Luri had laden it with berries and the sweet bursts in his mouth only made him crave the pastries more, but Luri had slapped his hand when he had reached for one.

"You'll be hungry by mid-morning," she had said. "Oats are more filling and you'll need your strength."

The test was set for midday, so Kieran didn't understand why he couldn't just have the oatmeal *and* a pastry, but Luri was adamant. She sat nibbling on a small piece of fruit. Kieran started to ask her why she didn't eat something more filling, but she interrupted him.

"I already did," she stated flatly.

"Gee, Luri, how long have you been awake?"

"Since before dawn." Luri suppressed a yawn. Kieran raised an eyebrow at her.

"I'm *fine*," she muttered, failing to stifle another yawn.

"It seems like we both could have gotten a little more sleep."

Before Luri could respond, several boys in red clothing approached their table. Kieran recognized the one Luri had pointed out last night, Artemael.

"Good morning," Artemael said silkily, extending a hand to Kieran. His skin was a golden tan and his dark bangs brushed across the top of his eyebrows. "We haven't met. I'm Artemael, son of Ervesh."

He said his father's name like it should mean something, but Kieran had never heard it before. Kieran returned the handshake.

"I'm Kieran," he said, adding no namesake. Artemael looked at him expectantly.

"Well," Artemael finally said once he realized Kieran wasn't going to say anything else. "My fellow Ignis and I would like to welcome you to the Academy."

"Thanks," Kieran replied. He looked over at Luri. She was sitting very stiffly.

"So I heard you were aiming for Clan Ignis," Artemael said snootily.

"Oh?" Kieran said, feigning surprise. "I don't remember telling anyone that."

A couple of the other Ignis students snickered. Artemael looked taken aback. He flicked his nose up in the air and glared down at Kieran and Luri.

"Perhaps I misheard," Artemael spat. "I had assumed you might have an ambition to rise to Sunfire.

Ignis is the clan that will get you there." Artemael smiled nastily and shifted his gaze to Luri. "However, if you would rather spend six years to change clans, you're on the right track."

Luri hung her head. Artemael motioned to his cackling followers, and they left. A tear welled in Luri's eye.

"Luri?" Kieran started to ask if she was okay. She waved him away and straightened herself.

"Don't let Artemael distract you," she said firmly. "Come on. It's time to meditate."

*   *   *   *   *   *

Kieran bent forward trying to catch his breath. Since breakfast, Luri had led them off to meditate, which Kieran found ridiculously boring, then to spar with Cortyn in a room with thin little mats. Cortyn had thrown Kieran to the ground and knocked the wind out of him several times. Then they went to the library for another study session and back to the dining hall for a snack. Kieran had hoped to snag a pastry, but the table had been cleared since breakfast. All that sat there now were some biscuits, dried meat, and some strange crunchy, green vegetables that Luri made Kieran eat. Last, they went outside for a run. Kieran started to sweat in the itchy, gray shirt. Finally, he caught his breath and looked up at Luri.

She was still fervently studying her checklist. She mumbled a time or two, something like, "Close enough," and "We don't really need that." Finally, the blasted journal snapped shut.

"I believe you're ready," Luri said proudly. "Even I wasn't this prepared."

"Great!" Kieran said through gritted teeth. *I think I'm going to hurl.*

"Just breathe," came Akiri's voice. Kieran laughed out loud.

"I've heard that from you before," Kieran spoke.

Luri looked at him curiously. "You've heard what before?"

Now Kieran really thought he would hurl. "Um…" he stammered. Before he had time to answer, a voice called out.

"Kieran of Tarmuth?"

Kieran turned and saw an older human woman searching for him. He raised his hand with a tiny jerk and made his way to her.

"I'm Kieran," he said nervously.

"I'm Madam Belva," she said tersely. Her blonde hair had flecks of gray and was perched atop her head in a painfully tight-looking bun. Her black tunic had a row of tiny silver buttons running from her chin to her waist. She had the straightest posture Kieran had ever seen.

"Young mage, please follow me. It is time for your evaluation test."

Kieran took one final look at Luri. She mouthed the words "good luck" as he started off after Madam Belva.

Chapter Eight
Face to Face

Madam Belva led Kieran to a large wooden chair in an empty, cavernous room. Kieran sat down and flexed his hands and feet nervously as he tried to remember the meditation techniques he had learned with Luri.

Kieran controlled his breathing and closed his eyes. His eyelids abruptly shot back open. It wasn't working. He hopped down from the large chair and started pacing around the room. The floor and walls were both made of stone.

To keep untrained flame wielders from burning down the place, Kieran thought. The same reason that there were no rugs or tapestries of any sort. Also, the room was lit not with torchlight, but panels of bright Moonstone.

Kieran recalled having drawn energy from the Moonstone that had been in his cell. He still didn't know how that had been possible, but assumed Akiri might have had something to do with it.

As Kieran continued walking around, his eyes fell on a strange object in the middle of the room. It was a jagged hunk of black slate nearly as big as Kieran himself. Unable to contain his curiosity, Kieran strode up and reached out tentatively.

"Wait!" Akiri's voice was sharp, but it was too late. Kieran's hand made contact with the smooth, cool stone.

Streaks of bright green light shot out of the stone, glowing with a supernatural light. The light rose up from the stone and materialized in the air.

The light took form in front of Kieran and he gasped. It was as if there was a person standing before him composed entirely of magic.

The being had an eerie greenish-blue glow. Magic pulsated through its entire form. It moved a step closer to Kieran and realization struck.

"Akiri!" Kieran cried out, amazed. The being gave a subtle nod, then suddenly a bright flash engulfed the room. The intensity of the light blinded Kieran. He raised his arm to cover his eyes.

The piece of slate was no longer in front of him. Also, the room was no longer empty. Kieran's heart pounded as he looked to see about twenty teachers now in the room. Soft murmurs floated through those in attendance. Some scribbled notes on parchment.

How are they here? Kieran panicked. *Akiri, did they see you?*

Akiri gave no answer. Kieran's eyes fell on Master Hartlan. Hartlan wore an almost amused expression, but it quickly faded from his face and he cleared his throat.

"The first test is complete," Hartlan said loudly. A couple of the others clapped softly, but most just looked on with perplexed expressions.

How was that a test? Kieran wondered. *I don't even know what I did. What was that stone?*

"Now to the second test," Hartlan announced. "Proficiency with the elemental artes. Master Fiora, are you ready?"

A short, wide human woman stepped forward and nodded. She had unkempt fuzzy brown hair and a pointed cap on her head. She wore long, flowing robes of emerald green with sleeves so long she had to keep flicking them back above her wrists.

With an exaggerated swish, she raised her arms upward. A scream caught in Kieran's throat as he jumped out of the way of a giant rock that raised up from the floor. Master Fiora waved her hands slowly and smoothly so that the rock hovered in front of Kieran.

"Please move the rock, young mage," Master Fiora said.

Kieran's mind was still buzzing from his encounter with Akiri. He felt too overwhelmed to move.

I can't do earth magic! Kieran thought. *I don't know what she expects me to do!*

"Here," came Akiri's calm voice. "Lift your palms gently and direct them at the stone."

Kieran raised his hands just as Akiri had said. He took in a breath and gave a gentle push toward the rock. He didn't expect anything to happen, but the rock shot across the room, narrowly missing Master Fiora. She let out a squeak and dove out of the way. The rock hit the wall with such force that it shattered.

Several of the other instructors let out frightened

yells at the blast. Most had at least flinched, but not Master Hartlan. His arms were crossed, and Kieran began to feel anxious.

Well, I'm not good at earth magic, he thought to himself. Akiri was silent.

After everyone settled down, Hartlan called Master Kaya, the Aqua clan leader. Kieran was taken aback by her appearance. She stood tall like an elf, but tiny, shimmering scales covered her entire body. The scales were a bluish-purple hue. Her head was bald and her ears were long and pointed. She wore a billowing white dress that fluttered around her as she walked forward.

She's from the Reshmayan people, he thought, referencing the aquatic race. Kieran knew little of them, mostly that they were excellent water wielders that usually lived near or in the sea. It was rare for a Reshmayan to travel through Tarmuth.

"Are you ready for my test, young mage?" Master Kaya's voice was silky and soft, like gentle waves lapping at the shore. She fell into a wielding stance as another instructor came forward carrying a large, lidless vase. Master Kaya moved her hands gracefully through the air and water from within the vase flowed toward her. She directed it in a delicate dance that encircled her. Finally, she pushed her hands forward and directed the water at Kieran.

"Ready yourself," Akiri commanded. Kieran put his hands up again, but with less force. He felt a pressure in his palms as he connected to the magical force Master

Kaya was projecting.

Kieran pulled back against that force and nearly toppled Master Kaya. She jerked backward, barely maintaining her balance, and the water splashed onto the floor.

Well, it looks like I'm not a water wielder either, Kieran thought glumly.

There was less chatter after this test, but it still took a moment for the room to regain its composure. Finally, a noble-looking Sombrayn stepped forward.

"My turn," the elf said arrogantly.

That must be Kovesh, Artemael's brother, Kieran thought. He faced Kovesh with slight trepidation. He could already feel the heat emanating from the Ignis leader.

Suddenly, Kieran started to feel violently ill. He doubled over just as Master Kovesh manifested a serpent-like flame. It licked hungrily through the air toward Kieran.

"Raise up!" Akiri commanded. Kieran tried to move, but couldn't find the strength. Right before the flames consumed Kieran, they suddenly dissipated. Kieran looked up to see Master Kovesh looking very smug. Master Hartlan, however, looked rather stern.

"That concludes your test, young mage," Master Hartlan said firmly. He looked around the room at the other teachers.

"On behalf of the Order, I thank you all for your service to the students of this school and for bearing witness to this young mage's prowess. May good favor follow you all."

With that, the room was dismissed. Kieran watched as they filed out slowly. His heart sank.

Did I fail? Kieran wondered. He waited for the other teachers to leave, then anxiously walked up to Master Hartlan. The Academy leader was gathering up some loose parchment.

"What happens now?" Kieran asked nervously. "Do I get sent to a Clan?"

Hartlan stared down at the papers, refusing to look Kieran in the eye. "The heads of the Clans will confer and come to a decision. You will be informed once it is made. In the meantime, you should rest."

Hartlan left the room and a bewildered Kieran behind. Nothing at all was making sense. Kieran tried reaching out to Akiri, but was met was silence from him as well. He gave up and headed to his room.

Kieran had thought there might be a crowd of curious students outside the doors, but found no one lingering in the hall. He walked back to the student quarters without passing many students at all. They no longer seemed to notice Kieran.

Kieran walked past his room and knocked on Luri's door. There was no answer.

She must be in a class, Kieran thought. He went back to his own room.

Kieran paced his room nervously for some time before deciding to put away the clothes Pip had left for him yesterday. He also examined the small desk in the corner of the room. He found blank parchment, a quill, and other small items to use for classes.

Kieran finally bored with wandering the room and came to rest on the bed. He laid back and tried to nap, but his mind was still racing.

Finally, a knock startled Kieran from his reverie. A young Alderan elf with tight, blonde curls peered at him.

"Master Hartlan sent me to give you this," she said cheerfully. Kieran held out his hand, and she placed a small object in his palm. She gave him a wide smile, then turned on her heels and scurried off. Kieran opened his hand to find a small clan pendant.

It was gold.

Chapter Nine
A Shiny, New Pendant

Kieran turned the gold pendant over and over in his hand, tracing its curved symbols with his fingertips. *How did I get into Clan Sunfire?*

He replayed the events of the test again and again in his mind. It made no sense.

I smashed the rock, I dropped the water, and I couldn't even connect to the fire. How did I get placed in Clan Sunfire?

Kieran waited expectantly for Akiri to say something, but to no avail. Frustrated, He put the pendant in his pocket and headed for the dining hall. Kieran had missed lunch because of his test, and his stomach growled ferociously.

When Kieran entered the dining hall, a hush fell over the room. It seemed most of the students had already gathered for dinner. He slowly made his way into the room and the silence turned into a loud, excited hum.

"There he is!"

"Is it really true?"

"Do you believe he attacked Master Kaya?"

Kieran ignored the whispers and started to fix a plate. *I'll just grab some food and take it back to my room,* he thought.

Suddenly, silence fell over the room once more as Luri entered. She looked furious.

"Let me see it!" she snarled. "Where is it?"

"Where is what?" Kieran asked defensively, trying to shove the pendant deeper into his pocket.

"Your *pendant*," she hissed. She put one hand on her hip and the other stretched out just shy of Kieran's nose. "Let's have it, shall we?"

Sheepishly Kieran pulled the gold pendant from his pocket. Luri snatched it from his hand and examined it closely. She held it up to the light and closed one eye. She turned it over and ran her fingers over its surface. At last she handed it back to Kieran.

"Congratulations," she snapped, thrusting the pendant back into his hand. She turned her nose up in the air and stormed off. Kieran was left flabbergasted.

Why is she so angry?

Just when Kieran thought it couldn't get worse, Artemael and his cronies strolled up to him. They all glared menacingly at Kieran.

"Well, I'd like to know who you had to bribe to start in Clan Sunfire," Artemael sneered. "Seems like you have some powers of persuasion."

Kieran gritted his teeth. He wanted to smart off to Artemael, but he was surrounded by fellow Ignis members. Kieran felt very outnumbered.

"I just don't understand," Artemael said haughtily. "How does a street kid from Tarmuth waltz in here and earn a place in Sunfire on his first day? That's a bit of a *wild* turn of events, wouldn't you say?"

"If you're going to accuse me of something, Artemael, just do it!" Kieran spat angrily.

Artemael leaned in closer. Kieran felt the all-too-familiar swell of flame magic emanating from the young Sombrayn.

"I believe you know exactly what I'm saying. No one truly of the Order would do as you have done."

"Is there trouble here, Artemael?" a cool voice asked from behind the group of Ignis.

Artemael whipped around to face his brother, Master Kovesh. A wicked grin crossed Artemael's lips.

"None at all, brother," he replied. "I was just *congratulating* the new Sunfire." He signaled his followers and brushed past Kieran. Kovesh stayed staring directly at him.

"I suggest you make your way back for the night," Kovesh said, his dark eyes glittering maliciously. "The path of a Sunfire mage is... strenuous."

Kieran watched him walk away. He realized he was no longer hungry and began to make his way back to his bedroom.

As he walked down the hallway to the student rooms, he pulled the pendant out of his pocket again. Light from a nearby window shone across it.

What a mess, Kieran thought. *What am I supposed to do in Sunfire?*

"Congratulations on landing in Sunfire!"

Kieran turned toward the voice and spotted a Veshtu elf sitting in a windowsill. A stained glass scene was depicted in the window and the sun coming through it cast the elf in an odd red and orange light. He pushed off from his seat and landed in front of Kieran.

Though Kieran had not met him before, there was no denying who he must be. *He looks just like Luri,* Kieran thought. *This must be Shivyn.*

Shivyn was tall and thin, just like his sister, with the same white blonde hair. He pushed his scraggly bangs out of his face.

"Very ambitious of you, landing in Sunfire. It makes the rest of us slackers look bad," Shivyn said with a wink. "Guess my tunic brought you some luck after all!"

Kieran didn't know what to say, but luckily Shivyn didn't give him a chance to speak.

"I bet my sister is steaming," he said with a crooked grin.

"What makes you say that?"

"Lulu is an excellent student," Shivyn began. "She's very talented for her age, too, but that doesn't mean that her time here has been easy. She's had to work really hard to get into one of the upper clans."

"I didn't ask to be put in Sunfire," Kieran said defensively.

"Whoa, simmer down," Shivyn said with mock concern. "You've just joined Sunfire on your own merit, and that's something to be proud of. Luri just needs some time to see that too. She'll come around, don't worry!"

Shivyn started to walk off, but turned back to face Kieran. "Pin that on your shirt," he said. "Wear it with pride! Don't be afraid to let everyone see where you landed."

"He's right," Akiri spoke up as Shivyn disappeared from sight. "You mustn't let the opinions of others diminish your own accomplishments. You will be extraordinary in Clan Sunfire."

But how do you know? Kieran wondered. *I still don't even understand who you are or why you are here.*

"All in good time," Akiri responded.

Kieran sighed. He knew he wouldn't get any more answers from Akiri.

As he continued down the hall, Kieran noticed something sitting in front of his doorway. As he drew closer, he could tell it was a stack of books. Tucked into the top book was a small stack of papers. Kieran pulled them out.

The first was a formal letter of acceptance to Clan Sunfire. Kieran skimmed over most of its formal wording, but read aloud a small portion.

"All Clan related inquiries should be directed to the Clan Sunfire leader," Kieran read.

But I don't know who the Clan Sunfire leader is.

The next paper listed Kieran's classes. His eyebrows raised when he saw the long list. There were the physically related classes: Basic Forms, Self-Defense without Aid of Magic, and Endurance Training. Kieran didn't like the sound of the latter two. Then there were the elemental arte classes. Kieran thought his focus would be in fire, but he had classes listed for all three main artes: earth, water, and fire.

At the very bottom of the list was a class

scheduled for only once a week. All it said was "Sunfire Training with Clan Leader" with no description.

I wonder what that will be like, Kieran pondered.

Kieran glanced at the remaining papers. He found a map of the Academy showing the locations of all the classrooms.

Kieran carried the books into his room and set them on his desk. He carefully looked over the schedule to see which classes he would have in the morning.

"Basic forms, Beginning Water Artes, Endurance, and Manipulation of Flame," Kieran read aloud. He looked over his schedule. Sunfire Training was the last class of the week.

I guess I'll find out then what it's all about, he thought. Kieran stacked the papers and slipped them back into one of the books. He gathered the books he would need for tomorrow's classes and shoved them into a leather knapsack Pip had left for him.

Kieran pulled off the awful, scratchy gray shirt he had worn for his test and pulled on a softer red one. He then pulled back the blankets on his bed and slid into it. It had been a very long day.

Just as Kieran closed his eyes, he heard a tentative knock at the door.

"Who is it?" Kieran called out abruptly.

"It's me," came Luri's soft voice. Kieran got up and walked over to the door. He pulled it open and saw Luri standing there looking nervous. Her hair was in two long, loose braids instead of the tight bun from that morning.

"Can we go for a walk?" she asked timidly.

Kieran nodded, and they set off down the hallway together. They turned down a nearby corridor, walking in silence. Kieran wondered what was on Luri's mind. He started to ask, but she spoke.

"I'm sorry for how I behaved earlier," she whispered.

"It's fine," Kieran replied.

"No," Luri said. "It's not. I was very rude. You should be very proud of starting in Clan Sunfire."

Kieran said nothing as they continued to walk. Finally, Luri spoke up again.

"It's just that it took me so long to move Clans. I had never expected someone with no prior magical training to come in and land in such a lucrative clan."

"But I want you to know that I am excited for you," Luri continued. "Truly, I am."

They walked on for some time until they came to Luri's favorite place, the library. She waved Kieran inside. Even though it was late in the evening, several students were still in there with their heads crammed in books. Luri pushed Kieran past them to an empty table in the back of the room.

"So tell me all about it," Luri said in a rushed whisper.

"Tell you all about what?"

"Shh," Luri quieted him. She looked around to make sure no one was listening.

"Tell me about your test. What happened?"

"Well," he began, careful to keep his voice low.

He started recounting the elemental tests with the three masters. He told her of how he had smashed the rock in Master Fiora's test, how he'd unbalanced Master Kaya, and lastly how he had totally floundered against Master Kovesh. Luri was silent as stone.

"It's very odd," she said finally. "And I mean no offense, but it doesn't appear that you were very successful in any of your tests."

"That's how I feel too," Kieran agreed. "I don't understand how I got placed in Sunfire."

"Well, it seems Master Hartlan has an interest in you," Luri considered. "Perhaps that's why you were placed there."

"Why would that matter?"

Luri grinned. "Kieran, do you know who the leader of Clan Sunfire is?"

"No."

"Master Hartlan is the leader of the Academy, but he is also the leader of Clan Sunfire," Luri explained. "I wonder if he requested you personally."

"Can he do that?"

Luri shrugged. "I'm not sure, but if anyone could do something that might go against the rules, it would be Master Hartlan."

Kieran wondered what Luri meant, but was interrupted as the librarian approached their table.

"It's late," she said briskly. She looked over their empty table and motioned toward the door. "Perhaps another location would be more suitable for social purposes at this hour."

*   *   *   *   *   *

Kieran and Luri were both laughing when they reached the student quarters. Conversation had turned lighter, and it felt to Kieran as if he'd known Luri for a very long time.

Luri stopped and faced Kieran before they separated for the night.

"Kieran, I really am sorry for my behavior earlier. I…"

"It's okay," Kieran reassured her.

"I was afraid I didn't do a good enough job as your student guide."

"Don't worry about it," Kieran said. "I don't really need a guide, but I'd settle for a friend."

Luri's eyes brightened. "Of course! Good night, Kieran."

Chapter Ten
Friends and Foes

The sound of students in the hallway woke Kieran earlier than he liked. He kicked off the blankets and got grudgingly to his feet. Back in Tarmuth, Kieran wouldn't rise until much later.

Kieran met Luri for breakfast in the dining hall. They talked cheerfully, though Luri gave Kieran a disapproving glance when she spied the pile of sweet pastries on his plate.

"Let me see your schedule again," Luri said, wiping her mouth daintily with a napkin. "Hmm, Basic Forms. That's with Master Myron. He's *ancient*, but a very good teacher."

She continued over the list. "I have Endurance today also, so I will see you then, and... oh." Luri stopped. "I see you already have a class with Master Kovesh today."

"Is that a bad thing?" Kieran asked through a mouthful of pastry.

"Not exactly," Luri replied. "It's just that he has very high expectations. He's one of the newer teachers to the Academy, but he's already made quite a name for himself. All the Ignis students practically worship him."

"Yeah, and his baby brother too," Kieran said

sarcastically.

"Try not to get on Artemael's bad side," Luri warned. "It's not worth the amount of trouble he could cause you."

Once they finished breakfast, the two friends parted ways. Luri bounded off to an upper level water arte class. Kieran grabbed the school map and headed toward his first class.

He found it rather easily and stepped into a large room on the ground floor of the castle. Most of Kieran's classmates appeared to be about his age. Kieran noticed a Lycalian boy that stuck out.

"Hey," Kieran called out to him. "You're related to Pip, right?"

The Lycalian looked up from a book. "Yes," he said flatly. "He's my uncle."

"We saw you the other day," Kieran said, offering a hand. "I'm Kieran."

"Pembran," the boy replied. He ignored Kieran's hand and returned to his book. Kieran shrugged, but before he could say anything else, an old elven man stepped into the room.

Master Myron was ancient, just as Luri had said, though elves aged differently than humans and often lived nearly twice as long. Master Myron's skin was still relatively smooth and without age spots. He was bald, so it was difficult for Kieran to tell his heritage.

For such an advanced age, Master Myron glided into the room. He kept his eyes closed and took even, careful breaths as he moved. To Kieran's amazement, he navigated the room well without sight. When he came to the center of the room, he stopped.

"We will begin today's class with our open wielding forms," Master Myron said in a sleepy sounding tone. "Forms one through seven. Please begin."

Panicked, Kieran looked around the room as the other students settled into forms. He had no idea what to do.

"Psst," Pembran whispered. He had removed his glasses and set aside his book. He stood tall with his palms pressed together in front of him.

"Follow my lead," Pembran whispered. Kieran fell into a stance beside him. Master Myron's voice called out calmly.

"One... Two... Three... Four."

Each time they found a stance, Master Myron would call for the next. At first Kieran felt off balance, but as he drew in a breath, he felt a steadiness from within. He could feel Akiri's presence more naturally.

"Wielding forms are important for a young mage to master," Akiri explained to Kieran. "Some artes require us to search deep within ourselves, such as fire, and pull forth a source of energy. Others, like the water artes, require us to reach out and touch a force to take control of it. It is part of the delicate balance of magic."

Master Myron continued to call out varying forms. Kieran started to pick up the new stances more quickly. Before he realized it, Master Myron dismissed the class.

"Hey, thanks for helping me out," Kieran said to

Pembran. Pembran replied only with a nod. He put his glasses back on, picked up his book, and left the class.

Kieran checked his schedule. Beginning Water Artes with Master Kaya was next. Kaya's class also took place within the castle. Her classroom suited her subject well. Blue and green stained glass panes made the classroom appear as if it were underwater.

The class went well, Kieran supposed, but was rather uneventful. Master Kaya made no mention of Kieran's encounter with her during his test. She taught the class simple water wielding techniques. Kieran tried with little success to mimic Master Kaya's tasks.

Kieran was excited to meet Luri for Endurance. As Kieran approached a dusty field near the lake, he spotted Luri. She had changed into cropped pants and a sleeveless top. Her long hair was pulled back in a high ponytail. She jogged over to Kieran.

"Oh no!" she slapped her palm to her forehead. "I didn't remind you to change."

Kieran knew better than to ask why. As he looked around, he noticed that everyone was wearing lighter clothes.

"Aren't you cold?" Kieran asked. Spring was nearing, but it was still rather cool out.

"Trust me, you'll be grateful for the cooler weather," Luri replied.

"So let me guess," Kieran mused. "Endurance class is…"

"Running, mostly," Luri finished his sentence. She wore a sly grin. "It's one of my favorite classes."

Luri and Kieran looked up as a lean centaur made his way toward the students. Luri whispered his name, Veridan, to Kieran.

"Three laps around Lake Ayhona," Veridan said flatly. "Two circuits through Whisperwell Woods. At your ready."

Kieran waited for a signal, but suddenly the class bolted. Veridan took off in the lead, galloping ahead of the others. Luri let out a delighted giggle and broke into a full run. Kieran did his best to keep up with her, but quickly started to fall behind. He was more used to short sprints back in Tarmuth, particularly when someone had caught him nicking a loaf of bread.

The group started their laps around Lake Ayhona. Kieran stopped more than once to catch his breath or grasp at a stitch in his side.

Kieran willed himself onto the footpath through Whisperwell Woods.

I don't see what this has to do with magic at all, he grumbled to himself.

"A strong body is better prepared to handle a powerful magic," Akiri replied.

Is that why I get sick when I try to wield? Kieran asked grumpily. *Because I don't run enough?*

Kieran felt a pensiveness from Akiri. "No," Akiri murmured softly. "At least not completely."

What do you mean?

"Your body needs training, that much is true," Akiri said. "However, I sense something... darker."

Kieran wanted to ask Akiri to explain, but was

surprised by Luri suddenly appearing over his shoulder.

"Veridan permitted me an extra lap so you wouldn't finish alone," she said perkily.

"You didn't... have to run... extra for me," Kieran panted.

Luri was still grinning from ear to ear. "I don't mind at all." Her breath was smooth and even.

When Luri and Kieran finished their run, the rest of the class was already starting back to the castle.

"Luri?" Kieran asked. "I have a question for you."

"Sure! What is it, Kieran?"

"What does your magic feel like to you? I mean, what does it feel like when you wield?"

Luri paused and thought for a moment. "It feels like... like everything around me is quieter," she said. "All the buzzing thoughts inside my head fade away and I just focus on the magic."

"So you don't hear anything?" Kieran asked.

"No," she said quietly. "Those aligned with the Order don't hear anything from their magic. Those that have fallen from the Order and taken other paths might hear something, but I don't really know."

"You mean like Wilders?" Kieran asked.

Luri shivered. "I don't really like that word," she said. "A Wilder is someone who has fully removed themselves from the graces of the Order. They have let their magic consume them and make decisions for them." She looked curiously at Kieran. "What makes you ask?"

"I'm just trying to understand," he replied hastily.

Luri's sapphire eyes peered into Kieran's. She

finally broke the gaze.

"You'd better hurry," she said. "Your next class will start soon, and Master Kovesh does not tolerate tardiness."

*   *   *   *   *   *

The halls of the Academy were daunting to Kieran as he checked his map. *Yes, this is the way.* He turned a corner and found himself in a long corridor lit by copious torchlight. The walls danced with flames and Kieran felt like he was standing in the belly of a great inferno.

This has to be the place, he mused. He felt bolstered by the surrounding fire and pulled on the brass handle to open the door.

To Kieran's surprise, the room inside was nearly pitch black, save for a few glowing patches on the walls. The students inside were all nearly silent. They looked up as the door let out a final creak and Kieran stepped inside. The echoes of his footsteps were nearly deafening.

"Ah, there's our new Sunfire," came a sneering voice.

Great, Artemael's here, Kieran thought.

"I hear you *excel* with flame," Artemael said sarcastically, stepping closer to Kieran.

Kieran held his ground but didn't goad Artemael, though he wanted to.

Artemael stopped right in front of Kieran's nose and laughed. "Perhaps it was just too much for a little street urchin to handle, seeing a true Flamemaster at work."

Kieran's thoughts felt frozen, though his body wasn't. He drew back a fist and launched it directly at Artemael's face. Artemael tried to dodge, but Kieran made contact with his cheek. Artemael grabbed at his jaw and turned his glittering black eyes at Kieran.

"I'll end you for that!" he roared. With an effortless flick of his wrist, a flame sprang forth and danced in his palm. Kieran braced himself as Artemael threw it forward.

"Get your hands up!" Akiri yelled.

Kieran threw his hands in front of his face. Instead of being burned by the flames, they seemed to hover in front of his palms. Kieran felt the connection to the magic and raised his arms to his sides. The flames pulsed and grew. Artemael scrambled backward.

"Dismiss the fire, now!" Akiri commanded.

Kieran fought against the desire to teach Artemael a lesson and relented. He lowered the flames until they disappeared into tiny wisps of smoke. Suddenly a voice called from the far side of the room.

"Class does not begin until I am present!" the voice hissed. A hooded figure was descending a spiral staircase across the room. He walked nearer and shed his cloak. It was Master Kovesh.

Kovesh's black hair was neatly trimmed and less untamed than his younger brother's. His expression looked like a mix of glee and disgust.

"Who initiated such a display?" Kovesh demanded.

No one dared to answer. Kieran's heart skipped a

beat as he looked at the faces of his fellow students. All their eyes were squarely on him. Kovesh approached Kieran.

"Now, boy, I understand you have very limited knowledge of the ways of this Academy," Master Kovesh said. "However, I will not tolerate the misuse of the fire artes in my classroom. You are dismissed from today's lessons and you can be sure that Master Hartlan will be made fully aware of your actions here."

Kieran swallowed back a bitter reply, taking heed from the feeling of pause he felt from Akiri. He grabbed his books and turned for the door.

All the way back down the corridor, Kieran raged silently.

Stupid Artemael! he thought angrily. *This is all his fault!*

Kieran made it to the dining hall but realized he was in no mood to be around anyone else at the moment. He turned to leave and nearly knocked Luri over.

"I'm sorry," Kieran stammered. "I didn't see you."

"It's all right," Luri replied, surprised. "What happened in class? It shouldn't be over yet."

"Artemael happened," Kieran spat angrily. He slammed his books on the ground. Several students around him jumped.

Luri looked for a moment like she would scold him, but she took in a breath instead. "Here." She picked up his books and handed them back to him. "Let me get you some food. We'll take it to the library to eat."

"I don't want to go to the library," Kieran said stubbornly.

"Then we'll go somewhere else," Luri encouraged. "I know a place. Wait here."

Kieran replayed the incident over and over while he waited for Luri. After a few moments, she came back with a plate piled high. There were rolls, legs of roast chicken, and sweet fruit pastries.

"Come on," Luri said kindly. "Follow me."

Luri led Kieran away from the main floor and up a long flight of stairs. At the top, they came to a room with a large window. Luri set down the plate and opened the latch. Luri pushed the thin glass window open and stepped out onto part of the castle roof.

She held out a hand to Kieran. "Trust me," she said, and he reluctantly followed her. The evening air was crisp and cold. The sun was setting, and Kieran and Luri both sat down on the roof to watch it fade.

Neither said anything for a while. Kieran slowly chewed on a piece of chicken while Luri daintily ate a roll. Finally, she worked up the courage to ask him what happened.

Kieran recounted Artemael's display in the classroom and Master Kovesh's harsh words. He ranted angrily for several minutes before finally coming to a stop. He looked expectantly at Luri. She had her arms wrapped around her legs with her chin resting on her knees.

She finally spoke. "Kieran, there's something I need to ask you."

Kieran was surprised. He had expected her to say something, *anything* about his encounter in Master Kovesh's class. However, he nodded to her, and she took a breath.

"You asked me if I hear anything when I use my magic. Now I feel I must ask you the same. What do you hear?"

"I…" Kieran began. He looked into Luri's face and for the first time in his life, he felt like he was looking at a real friend. He took a deep breath and words poured out of him. He told her of feeling a presence, then how that presence gave its name. He spoke of feeling the urges and hearing Akiri guiding him. The entire time he spoke, Luri was silent. At last he stopped.

Luri sat there frozen for a long time. Finally, she started to stand.

"I don't know what all of this means," Luri said softly. "However, I know that I trust you. Now, come on. It's getting cold and you've had a long day."

Relieved that Luri hadn't turned on him, Kieran stood too. Luri was right. It had been a *long* day.

Chapter Eleven
Cursed or Cured?

The next morning before classes, Kieran was called into Hartlan's office. It was smaller than Kieran had thought it would be, and rather untidy for what he had expected from the leader of the Academy. The desk Hartlan sat at was piled high with messy stacks of parchment and books. Hartlan motioned for Kieran to have a seat opposite him in a scarlet chair.

"I heard you had quite the eventful first day," Master Hartlan said, not glancing up from the stack of papers.

"Yes sir," Kieran nodded. "But…"

Master Hartlan cut him off. "I understand you are new, so this time I will leave you with just a warning. However, I will not tolerate the attack of another student. And while I will not be assigning you any consequences, Master Kovesh has the dominion over the punishments the students of his classes incur."

Kieran's cheeks were red, and he hung his head. He stared at the papers on Hartlan's desk as the leader sorted through the stacks. As Hartlan lifted another piece of parchment, Kieran caught sight of a small, glittering crimson object. Before Kieran could discern what it was, another piece of parchment covered it.

"You are dismissed, Kieran," Hartlan said suddenly, startling Kieran from his thoughts. He rose quickly to his feet and left the office. Master Hartlan's change in attitude confused him; he had been so open and warm when Kieran had first met him. Now he seemed harsh and distant.

The next few days went with little incident, save for Master Kovesh's class. When Kieran returned to it, he was promptly pulled aside by Kovesh and given a three-week suspension from wielding in his class. Kieran watched from the back of the room as his classmates conjured and manipulated fire. Artemael looked especially pleased with Kieran's punishment, as he had not received one of his own.

By the end of his first week at the Academy, Kieran was exhausted, but curious of his clan-specific training with Master Hartlan. He wondered how Master Hartlan would act toward him.

Still relying on the map, Kieran navigated the halls to find the Sunfire training room. The walls of the room were adorned with gold banners of the clan's color, but was lacking in other decorations. It felt plain compared to other classrooms like Master Kaya's or Kovesh's.

Kieran walked over to a table with three other young Sunfires and found a seat. Before he could introduce himself, an older Alderan student stepped to the front of the classroom. He had short coppery-brown hair and long, elven ears.

"For the newer students that may not know me, I am Tersha." the student said loudly. "I'm in my twelfth year of study here at the Academy. Unfortunately, Master Hartlan cannot attend the Beginner's class for Clan Sunfire today and has sent me in his stead. Now, if you will all turn to Chapter Eight of your textbooks and read through Chapter Twelve. When you have finished, you may be excused from class."

Disappointed, Kieran pulled out the text for the class, *Mages and Their Place in the Order,* and turned to Chapter Eight. The room was silent except for the swish of turning pages as each of the students settled in to read. Tersha made his way to a large chair at the front of the room and sank into it.

Kieran skimmed the dry passages, feeling rather bored. He read of rules and expectations of the mages of the Order, of the history of such, but then a particular heading caught his eye.

"Midlings: Cursed or Cured?" Kieran began reading. A vague figure was depicted in full mage's robes. The face of the drawing was obscured and a shadowy presence hung in the air above the mage.

"Ever the enigma, Midlings have emerged throughout the history of Peria as mages of great power and ability." Kieran continued reading. "However, the sentience of the magical ability of a Midling has often led them down dark paths of destruction. Some have gained harmony and risen to places of honor, though many in the

Order believe the very existence of such a presence endangers the world."

Midling? Kieran thought. *Akiri, is that why I can hear you? Am I a Midling?*

"That may be your word for it," Akiri replied. "I do not always understand the words of your kind."

Kieran waited for a few more moments until the other students started to leave. Finally, Kieran grabbed his books and took off to find Luri.

Kieran found her coming out of a Healing Artes class looking frustrated. He caught her attention, and she made her way to him.

"Oh, hi Kieran," Luri said, sounding a bit distracted.

"Luri, I found something I need to show you," Kieran said excitedly. "Just not here."

Luri followed Kieran to their table in the back of the library. He opened the book and flipped to the page about Midlings. He waited impatiently as Luri read. Finally, she looked up.

"I've heard of Midlings before," Luri said pensively. "However, I don't really know much about them."

"It makes sense, though," Kieran said, pointing back to the passage. "This has got to be why I can hear Akiri."

"There's still so much to learn," Luri said, sounding tired.

Kieran looked at his friend. Luri was usually full of energy, but for the first time since Kieran had met her,

Luri looked drained. She had dark circles beneath her eyes and she sat slumped in her chair.

"Luri, are you okay?"

"I'm fine," she stated weakly. "I've just been having some trouble with my healing classes, that's all."

"What kind of trouble?"

"It's nothing," Luri said, straightening in her chair. She took in a deep breath and changed the subject back to Kieran.

"It is interesting, what you have found," she said, trying to sound chipper. "I'll do some research and see what I can find out about Midlings."

"Thanks, Luri."

*   *   *   *   *   *

The next couple of weeks went by quickly as Kieran started to settle into his new routine at the Academy. Winter's cold chill started to give way to warm spring breezes that made Endurance class slightly more bearable. Kieran and Luri spent their runs together now, and he found it a little easier to keep up with her.

Kieran was having small successes with his earth and water arte classes as well. Master Kaya had actually smiled one day after Kieran had successfully drawn water from a pitcher by magic.

Master Kovesh's class was another story, and Kieran continued to feel frustrated as he finished out his suspension. The third week finally passed, and Kieran woke up excitedly on the next day.

Today's the day.

Kieran's heart pounded with excitement as he

piled his plate with pastries at breakfast. Nervous beads of sweat dotted his brow as he exerted magical energy in his early classes. At last, it was time, and he strolled confidently down the fiery corridor that led to Master Kovesh's classroom. The flames surged as Kieran drew near. He encouraged their ebb and flow by raising and lowering his hands as he walked.

"I'd be careful of that, if I were you," a voice sneered from the doorway. Kieran looked up to see Artemael and his fellow Ignis blocking the entrance to the classroom.

Artemael eased off the doorway and walked toward Kieran. Again the flames surged, though this time Kieran didn't intend for them to.

"Go on," Artemael spat an inch from Kieran's face. "Rain it down, I dare you! Call down the fire! Give in, *Wilder*!"

"Don't call me that!" Kieran snapped, pushing Artemael away. "If there's a Wilder here, it's you!"

Artemael's friends cackled, and Artemael himself let out a laugh. "You really are lost, street kid. My family has faithfully served in the Order for ages! You will learn your place when you speak to me!"

Artemael raised his knee swiftly and caught Kieran in the stomach. The wind was knocked from him and Kieran crumpled to his knees.

"That," Artemael hissed in Kieran's ear, "is your due for your past actions against me. Learn your place or find that you no longer have one."

Artemael straightened and headed to the

classroom. He stopped and turned back to Kieran.

"It would be a shame for you to be late," Artemael said with a slimy grin. "After all, you've waited *so long* for a chance to wield."

Artemael walked off, laughing. Kieran rose from the ground, steaming.

What a little...

Akiri's calm voice rang out.

"He's not worth it. Don't let him rattle you. This is your day. It is finally time for you to train in the fire artes."

Kieran tried to steady himself, but found his anger pulsing in time to the flickering flames in the hall.

Finally, Kieran walked to the door and stepped inside. Master Kovesh was already standing before the students looking rather unhappy. To his right, looking equally unpleasant, stood Master Hartlan with his arms crossed.

What's he doing here? Kieran wondered.

"Students," Master Kovesh began tensely. "Today we have the pleasure of having our Academy Leader among us to observe your progress. Today's lesson will be more of an evaluation of the skills you've learned thus far."

Great! Kieran thought darkly. *I haven't had the chance to train at all!*

Kieran had been watching the movements from the last few weeks of classes and practicing some in secret, but never by conjuring his own flame. So far he had only ever manipulated an existing flame, except for the time while traveling to the Academy.

At Kovesh's direction, the students assembled in a line. Kieran tried to move to the very back, but Artemael blocked his way with a wicked grin.

"I know how long you've waited for this moment," Artemael chided. "Go on in front of me. That way, when you fail to produce even an ember, I can show you how a *proper* fire mage wields!"

"Stay calm," Akiri urged. "Do not worry. I will be here to help you."

One by one, the students came before Master Kovesh. He set them forth tasks. Kieran watched as mostly Ignis students produced various manifestations of flames. There were a few others from Clan Sunfire like him, and they too performed their tasks.

Finally, there was only one Ignis student left in line before Kieran. The familiar pounding in his ears ensued and heavy waves of fear and anger washed over him. He watched his classmate raise his hands and call forth embers. They danced delicately at his fingertips. Master Kovesh murmured to the student, and the fire vanished.

"Kieran of Tarmuth," Master Kovesh called dryly.

Kieran stepped forward. Master Kovesh turned to Master Hartlan.

"As you are aware, *this* student has not been permitted to wield flame due to a previous incident."

"I would still like to see his ability," Master Hartlan said firmly. He locked eyes with Kieran for a moment. Kieran felt very nervous.

"Very well," Kovesh glared. "Step forward, young mage. Let's see if you've been paying attention. I want to see you call forth a flame."

"Perhaps that is beyond his current scope," Hartlan interjected. "An untrained mage is better suited to manipulate rather than manifest on his first attempt."

Kovesh shot Master Hartlan a look of contempt. He snapped his gaze back to Kieran.

"Prepare yourself, young mage!" Kovesh bellowed. Before Kieran could react, Kovesh had produced a long, flickering flame. He directed it through the air toward Kieran. Kieran put up his hands to connect with the flame.

As Kovesh's magic made contact with Kieran, he was hit with the same dizzying sickness from before. Kieran's head throbbed and his chest ached.

"Steady!" Akiri called out. "Push the flow away from you!"

It felt as if the magic would nearly consume him. Kieran's vision started to blur.

Kieran pushed with all his might and urged the flame to move from him. It crackled through the air, causing his classmates to cower. Even Artemael dropped to his stomach on the floor.

Something felt strange, yet invigorating to Kieran. He caused the flame to rise and fall throughout the room with large sweeping movements of his arms.

"Be careful!" Akiri warned. "You are losing control of the fire!"

The magic felt to Kieran like it had a life of its

own. He tried to heed Akiri's warning and dismiss it, but it raged stronger instead. Kieran's mind started to feel fuzzy.

Kovesh demanded that Kieran stop, but instinctively Kieran raised his hands and the flame surged more. He faintly felt Kovesh trying to regain control and Kieran fought back against him. Finally, Master Hartlan stepped in.

"That's enough, Kieran!" he roared, raising his hands. In an instant, the flames vanished. Kieran finally snapped out of it and looked around the room. The students looked at him fearfully and Kovesh leaned against the wall sweating and panting.

After a moment, Kovesh straightened himself, looking livid. He came toward Kieran with a finger raised angrily. He opened his mouth to speak, but Master Hartlan interrupted him.

"I think that is all for today's class," Hartlan stated firmly. "Students, you are dismissed."

Kieran watched as his classmates filed out of the room. Artemael gave Kieran a wild-eyed look before exiting. Kieran stayed put.

Why does this keep happening? Kieran asked Akiri.

Akiri was silent. Kieran thought about asking Master Hartlan, but as he approached, Master Hartlan urged him to the door.

Confused and frustrated, Kieran stormed off. He raged at Artemael, Kovesh, and Hartlan in his head and wasn't watching where he was walking. He turned a corner too quickly and knocked Luri to the ground.

"I'm sorry," Kieran muttered, reaching out a hand to Luri.

"It's all right," Luri said, dusting herself off.

"What are you doing here?"

Luri gave him a puzzled look. "I wanted to see how your class went. I know it was a big day for you."

Kieran took a deep breath and shared what a total disaster the class had been.

"Luri," Kieran said, his voice getting quieter. "Something was wrong. I couldn't control the fire, and I don't think it's because I'm not trained. And I don't think it's because of Akiri either, because he was trying to help me. It felt like something else."

Luri seemed to think for a minute. "I've been trying to learn more about Midlings," she finally said. "From what I've read, Midlings can be more sensitive to the magic of others. If there was someone outside of the Order around, you might notice it more acutely."

"You mean if a Wilder was around?" Kieran asked.

Luri nodded. "A Wilder at the Academy would be very bad news. The Order would likely conduct an investigation. Master Hartlan already isn't in the greatest of favor with the Order."

"Why is that?" Kieran asked curiously.

"His ways are... different," Luri explained. "Master Hartlan believes the Order has held onto the ancient beliefs and has not changed with the times. He believes that history, just like the magic within us, ebbs and changes."

"Well, he's right."

"Maybe so," Luri pondered, "but that isn't the way of the Order. The Order believes in absolutes: that a rule made should never be broken, regardless of the circumstance."

"All I know," Luri continued, "is that Master Hartlan has bent the rules, even if the Order is not aware of it, by admitting a Midling to the Academy. It wouldn't be a far stretch to think that he could allow in a Wilder. Has he seemed strange during your Clan Sunfire classes?"

"He's still been sending that older student, Tersha," Kieran said glumly. "I haven't seen Master Hartlan in class at all. We're just having to read from stupid history books. I thought I'd be learning to wield or something!"

"Don't take those history books for granted," Luri said seriously. "Learning from the past can be very important for the future. Speaking of such, I also read that a Midling and his magical force should practice together to strengthen their connection."

"I'll get on that, seeing as I have so much free time as a Sunfire," Kieran said sarcastically.

Luri ignored him and the two walked in silence the rest of the way back to their rooms. Luri bid Kieran good night and disappeared into her bedroom. Kieran remained standing in the hall turning Luri's words over and over in his head. Something was bothering him.

Akiri?

"Yes?" Akiri answered.

I have a question for you. Can you feel when a Wilder is near?

"At times," Akiri replied. "It's not always exact. I can only feel a Wilder when they are actively accessing their magic."

Did you feel a Wilder today? Kieran prodded.

"Yes. I just don't know who it was."

Chapter Twelve
Whispers of Wilders

Akiri's words haunted Kieran all night. His mind was restless, and he barely slept. The next morning, he and Luri tried to gain more answers.

"So Akiri doesn't know who the Wilder is?" Luri whispered.

"No," Kieran said, breathing hard. The two were running the familiar paths during their Endurance class.

"But he could sense it was someone in the room," Luri said. "So that narrows it down. Who do you think would be the most likely?"

"Artemael," Kieran said immediately. "You know he attacked me before class started."

"Artemael's a bully, there's no doubt of that," Luri said. "However, I've seen Artemael wield, and honestly he's not that good. If his brother wasn't the head of Ignis, Artemael wouldn't have any clout at all."

"Okay," Kieran thought. "Then maybe it's Kovesh. He's very skilled."

"I really don't think it could be Artemael or Kovesh," Luri stated. "Their entire family is very dedicated to the Order."

"Then who do you think it is?" Kieran asked.

Luri looked nervous. "I think it might be Master

Hartlan."

"No way! He's the leader of the Academy!"

"I know," Luri said. "But think about it for a moment. When you were before the Keepers, you got sick, just as you said you did when you were traveling to the Academy, and during your evaluation. And who was there all of those times?"

"Master Hartlan," Kieran answered solemnly. "But I just don't see how..."

"And think, Kieran," Luri went on. "Master Kovesh noticed something at your test and has been watching you closely. Was he happy about Master Hartlan observing his class?"

"Well, of course he wasn't," Kieran replied.

"I think Master Kovesh suspects Master Hartlan," Luri said. "He can't say anything without proof, though. I bet he is working for the Order."

"And what would that mean?"

"It would mean that the Order is probably about to get more involved at the Academy," Luri answered. "They will probably send delegates to investigate the school."

Kieran didn't like the sound of that. "What if they find out that I'm a Midling?"

Luri looked at him gently. "Just lie low. And try to stay away from Master Hartlan. In the meantime, you and Akiri need to practice together. If he really is a presence from long ago, I'm sure he will have interesting things to share with you."

*   *   *   *   *   *

Kieran went about his classes the next few days with a feeling of dread and uncertainty. He tried to heed Luri's advice and keep attention off of himself, but he had already attracted a lot of notice.

In the meantime, Kieran took his sparse free moments and tried to get to know Akiri better. The more they talked, the more like a real person Akiri seemed.

I still feel strange talking to you, Akiri, Kieran said to his magic. *I feel like I'm talking to myself.*

"I am a part of you, so that sentiment is partly true."

But we're so different! I just don't get it!

"We're all more alike than you think," Akiri said. "Close your eyes for a moment." Kieran hesitantly obliged.

"Now, imagine that your magic is a line. Feel for it."

Kieran felt a little silly, but he complied. He imagined an orange line glowing with the heat of fire magic. It rippled like a wave with sharp, quick movements.

"Now, see if you can feel mine."

Kieran sensed Akiri's line. Its hum was slow and steady.

"If we can bring our rhythms together, we'll achieve a power that few mages ever experience in their lifetime."

Kieran tried to get his own magical pulse to match Akiri's, but he couldn't seem to slow down his rhythm. He felt frustrated.

"It will take us much time and practice," Akiri said reassuringly.

Kieran tried to practice with Akiri, but his mind still raced each time with worries of what would happen should the Order come to the Academy.

At the end of the week, Luri's warning of the Order's imminent presence seemed to come true. As Kieran went to Master Kovesh's class, he noticed the door was ajar. He could hear the buzz of voices coming from within. They appeared to be gathered around something.

The students fell immediately silent as Kieran entered the room. A few gave him worried looks.

"What's going on?" Kieran asked a short Ignis girl. She pointed to a piece of parchment on the wall. Kieran moved closer to read it.

"By decree of the Order of Peria, students in pursuit of the technique of the arte of flame shall no longer be permitted to conjure of their own volition, but instead may only manipulate flames of a small source."

Instead of the large, empty space they usually practiced in, tables had been moved in and set with small candles. Disgruntled comments came from the older more experienced students.

An Ignis centaur pushed his way forward. "It's all this one's fault!" he said angrily, pointing at Kieran. "He can't control his magic so now we're all going to be set back to beginner levels!"

"Be settled, Palter," Master Kovesh said, coming to the center of the room. He motioned for the students to gather around.

"As you can all see," Kovesh called out to the room. "The Order has found it necessary to set precautions in place for the protection of the students of this illustrious Academy. Henceforth, you will find that my class will be keeping in accordance with these new rules."

Several students groaned. Master Kovesh raised a hand to quieten them.

"I understand the frustrations you must be feeling," Master Kovesh said. "However, the safety of all of our students, both old and new..." Kovesh looked directly at Kieran, "is of the utmost importance."

"Now," he continued. "You will each select a table and a candle. Once all are ready, I will lead the class through the basic steps of flame manipulation."

The students moved to the tables. Kieran found himself at a table alone. *Just as well,* he thought.

Master Kovesh talked the class through the basic steps. Kieran had no trouble manipulating the flame to grow larger or smaller, or move from side to side. He looked over to where Artemael was practicing. Artemael looked aggravated and was waving his arms rapidly over a flame that barely moved.

Kieran continued to practice and soon realized that he did not feel the strong welling in his chest or a headache. It should have made Kieran happy, but instead it made him fear that Luri was right.

What if Master Hartlan is a Wilder? Kieran asked Akiri.

"I don't know," Akiri answered. Kieran could feel that Akiri was distracted, but he didn't pursue it.

Class ended without incident, and Kieran soon learned that Master Kovesh's class was not the only one affected by change. All the teachers were making subtle changes to their teaching methods. The changes at the Academy became even more clear at breakfast the following morning when Master Hartlan appeared in the dining hall.

"That's odd," Luri whispered to Kieran. "Master Hartlan rarely makes announcements."

Hartlan stood before the students with several of the other Academy teachers at his side. Kieran noticed a few unfamiliar faces as well and one that stood out.

"I know him!" Kieran whispered to Luri, pointing out a Sombrayn guard with a crescent-shaped scar on his cheek. "That's Caydn. He was one of the guards in Tarmuth."

"If I may have your attention, please," Master Hartlan began, clearing his throat. "I'm sure most of you are aware of the new ordinances being set forth by the Order of Peria. Here to further expand upon the Order's newfound involvement is Seeker Tula."

A Veshtu woman glided forward. Her long white hair was tightly braided over her left shoulder. Her blue eyes scanned the room of students.

"Fine students," Seeker Tula began softly. "The Order of Peria sends its highest regards to each of your esteemed teachers." She gave a graceful nod of her head to the Academy staff. "The Order also wishes to commend the discipline and tenacity shown throughout the ages by the students that grace these halls."

"We do not wish to interrupt the instruction you receive," she continued. "However, it has come to the attention of the Order that there is cause for more stringent precautions to be put in place. By decree of the high council, the delegation for the preservation of the integrity of magical artes shall take up residence here at this present time."

Kieran turned to Luri. "What in the world did all of that mean?"

"It means," Luri whispered hastily, "that the Order has sent delegates to watch us."

"... And to watch the teachers," a familiar voice said behind them. Luri jumped and turned around.

"Shivyn!" she exclaimed. "You scared me half to death! Don't do that!"

Shivyn gave his customary teasing grin and cast a wink at Kieran. "So what are we going to do about this, Lulu?"

Luri stiffened at the nickname. "Do not call me that, Shivyn," she said through gritted teeth. "And there's nothing for us to do except to keep ourselves out of trouble."

"Easy for you," Shivyn said playfully. He pointed to himself and Kieran. "Not so simple for the rest of us."

"Well, you're both going to have to try!" Luri said indignantly.

Shivyn ruffled Luri's hair playfully and rose from the table. Luri shot him a disdainful look as he bounded off.

She turned back to Kieran and spoke in a whisper. "With the Order's presence here, it's only a matter of time before something happens."

"But isn't the Order here because of me?" Kieran asked. "I'm the one who nearly lost control in Kovesh's class. Why don't they just arrest me?"

"They know it must be more than that," Luri answered. "No offense, Kieran, but what happened in Master Kovesh's class was more advanced than what a new mage can do on their own, even for a Sunfire. Something else is going on, and the Order has come to find out what."

"Do you think it could have anything to do with what happened in Tarmuth?" Kieran asked, looking again to where Caydn stood. The Flamemaster was looking at Kieran as well.

"Maybe," Luri said. "You still can't remember anything?"

"Nothing from before I was captured by the guard." Kieran turned his gaze back to his friend. "It was so weird though. There was so much fire. I've never seen the Sombrayns lose control of the torches like that."

"It had to be someone very powerful," Luri said. "I just wonder why they did it."

*   *   *   *   *   *

"Kieran, *please* pay attention!"

Kieran's head jerked at the sound of Master Kaya's voice.

"I'm sorry, Master Kaya," Kieran mumbled.

Master Kaya watched Kieran carefully for a moment and then continued her instructions to the class. Kieran's mind started to drift off again.

He tried his best to recall what had happened in Tarmuth, but it was still no clearer than before.

Akiri? Kieran asked tentatively. *Do you know why someone would start such a large fire in the city?*

"I'm sure there are many reasons," Akiri began. "Perhaps it was to attack someone."

That doesn't make sense, Kieran replied, thinking hard. *There would have been reports if someone had been injured.*

"Then perhaps it was a distraction," Akiri said.

A distraction from what?

"That is unclear," Akiri stated. Kieran thought for a while about what it could be. Suddenly, his thoughts flashed back to Hartlan's office and the strange ruby object on his desk.

Could Hartlan have stolen something from Tarmuth? Kieran wondered. Suddenly, a wet slap jolted him from his thoughts.

As Kieran sputtered, several of his classmates let out a snicker. His hair and clothing were absolutely soaked. Master Kaya walked over to Kieran looking rather unhappy.

"Young mage!" she said, her usually fluid voice holding more of a bite. "You were supposed to deflect the water!"

"Looks like he deflected it with his face!" an elven boy laughed.

Master Kaya gave the boy a stern glance. "This is a good place to end today's lesson."

As the others started to leave, Kieran slipped to the back of the room. There he found some thin towels that he used to dry himself.

Kieran finished and started to gather his things when someone entered the room. Kieran ducked down in the back of the room behind some desks. He peered up to see Flamemaster Caydn approaching Master Kaya.

"Greetings, Master Kaya," Caydn said formally. Master Kaya returned the greeting with a small nod of her head.

"What can I do for you, Flamemaster Caydn?" she asked tersely. She started putting away materials from her class and did not look up at her visitor.

"I was hoping that you had located the... *item* in question," Caydn said quietly.

"I would have alerted you if I had," Master Kaya replied. "I fear the tracking magic has been altered. I don't believe I will be able to offer much assistance."

"You are aware of the gravity of this situation," Caydn said sternly. "Should the seal be broken as well…"

"Oh, I am very well aware," Master Kaya snapped. "You need not explain the repercussions to me, Caydn."

"My apologies," Caydn offered a slight bow.

Kieran watched Caydn exit the room. He stayed silent as Master Kaya then finished collecting her things and left.

Akiri, I think you were right about a distraction,

Kieran thought, his heart thudding in his ears. *I think someone stole something from Tarmuth and brought it to the Academy.*

Akiri was his usual silent self, so Kieran waited until he knew for sure both Master Kaya and Caydn were gone. With his heart still pounding, he bolted from the room.

Chapter Thirteen
Founders' Tale

Kieran raced through the crowded halls to find Luri. *Something's going on,* Kieran thought. He started to realize there were far more students out than usual.

At last, Kieran reached the healing classroom where Luri was having class. Master Rellus stood in the doorway shooing students away. He noticed Kieran, however, and waved him forward. Confused, Kieran approached.

"You're Luri's friend," Master Rellus said quietly to Kieran. Curious students still pressed around them.

"Yes," Kieran replied, looking up at the Clan Moonglow leader.

"Come inside," Master Rellus said, opening the door just wide enough for Kieran to step in. He walked through hesitantly.

Master Rellus' healing classroom was a quiet, restful place. The runic lights in the ceiling were a gentle blue hue, and a runed water feature sat in the corner. Kieran watched as the water trickled in an infinite loop, resonating softly through the room.

"I'm afraid your friend has fallen ill," Master Rellus said gently. Kieran looked up into his icy blue eyes. Judging by his curly ginger hair, Master Rellus was an Alderan elf.

"Is Luri okay?" Kieran asked worriedly.

"She is," Master Rellus replied calmly. "She overexerted her magic in class and fainted. She just needs some rest. I believe seeing a friendly face would help her recover as well."

Kieran nodded and Master Rellus led him through an adjacent door. Inside there, the lights bathed the room in a bright white light. Beds with pale mint sheets were lined against the wall.

"Is this the recovery wing?" Kieran asked, luckily having not had to visit it yet.

"Yes," Master Rellus replied. He pointed to a bed at the far end of the room. "Your friend is resting there."

Kieran nodded his thanks and started toward Luri. He passed several older Moonglow students wearing teal tunics. They walked up and down the aisle checking on the students in the beds.

Kieran reached Luri and sat in a chair beside her. She was sitting up sipping some sweet juice. She was pale and her long hair looked unkempt for the first time since Kieran had met her.

"Are you okay, Luri?" Kieran asked.

"I'm fine," Luri answered, her voice a little weaker than normal. "I just pushed myself too hard."

Luri started coughing and one of the Moonglow students came over and gave her a cool cloth. Kieran sat beside her feeling useless. Finally, as her coughing subsided, she spoke.

"Really, I'm fine, Kieran," she said. "You should

go to dinner."

"I already ate," Kieran lied, not wanting to leave her. "You just lay back and close your eyes, okay? Don't worry about me."

Luri gave a weak grin and settled against the pillows. She closed her eyes and drifted off to sleep.

Kieran settled into the chair for the night. It felt strange to Kieran, to have someone to be worried about.

After a short time, Master Rellus brought Kieran a plate of food.

"You must be hungry," the teacher said kindly.

Kieran took the food and happily dove into it. Master Rellus sat down in a chair on the other side of Luri. Kieran watched as Master Rellus gently lifted Luri's wrist and checked her pulse. She didn't stir.

"She will feel much better in the morning," Master Rellus said to Kieran. "She's a very talented young mage, but is a bit too hard on herself."

"What do you mean?" Kieran asked through a mouthful of potatoes.

"Luri pushes herself more than most students her age," Rellus replied. "Most students don't enter the Academy until they are older. Luri has accomplished much in her time here, but she doesn't always see it. Her ambition has created a divide between her and most of her classmates. I'm glad she has found a friend in you, Kieran."

Me too, Kieran thought, grateful to have Luri by his side. His mind raced back to his revelation in Master Kaya's class, and though he ached to tell Luri, he pushed it down.

*   *   *   *   *   *

"Are you still sleeping?"

Luri's voice startled Kieran awake, and he nearly fell out of his chair. Luri let out a little giggle as Kieran stumbled to his feet.

"How are you feeling?" he asked her, trying to regain his composure.

"Much better," Luri smiled. Her color had returned to her cheeks and her hair was neatly pulled back. She sat upright in the bed in front of a pile of open books.

"Are you studying?" Kieran asked, thinking that was the last thing he'd be doing in her situation.

"Yes," Luri replied. "Master Rellus wants me to take the day to rest, so I don't want to fall behind."

Kieran thought back to Master Rellus' conversation and realized that Luri would not be swayed.

"Well, I can stay and help you study," Kieran said seriously. Luri laughed.

"Oh no," she said. "You're not skipping classes on my behalf."

"Well, it's not without reason," Kieran began. "I really need to tell you something."

Luri leaned in, but before Kieran could talk, one of the student healers came up to check on her.

"You can tell me later," Luri whispered. "Now, go to class!"

*   *   *   *   *   *

Kieran couldn't focus at all during his classes. He

stood in the back in Master Myron's Forms' class, faking the motions of the wielding forms. Pembran shot him several disapproving looks, though Kieran was too preoccupied to notice.

What could they be looking for, Akiri? Kieran wondered, raising his right leg and sweeping out his arm as Master Myron neared him. *It has to be important for the Order to have become so involved.*

"It must be something powerful," Akiri said. "A Wilder typically desires sources of great power."

But that means it could be anything! Kieran brought his leg down and exhaled.

"Not so," Akiri replied. "Only certain magical objects would hold an interest for a Wilder."

We need to narrow it down, Kieran bent his knees and pushed his hands out in front of him.

"Luri might have answers," Akiri said.

Yeah, if I can ever talk to her! Kieran let out a grunt as he nearly toppled over. Kieran made it through the rest of Forms and hurried to his Sunfire class.

Kieran had to suppress a groan as he noticed Tersha once again at the front of the classroom.

Where is Master Hartlan? Kieran wondered. *Is he ever going to show up?*

Kieran settled into his seat at the back of the class. The last thing he felt like doing was thumbing through more boring old texts. Just as he started to come up with an excuse to leave early, Tersha cleared his throat.

"Please join me in welcoming our newest member to Clan Sunfire!" he said enthusiastically. Kieran craned his neck to look over the rows ahead of him. Beside Tersha stood an unfamiliar elven girl.

"This is Ayomi," Tersha continued. "She has just transferred from clan Ignis. I hope you will all help her feel welcome!"

The other Sunfires offered polite greetings. Ayomi gave a small wave and tucked a piece of her long, ebony hair behind her ear. Tersha motioned for her to find a seat. Kieran's heart quickened as she came to the back of the room. Ayomi slid gracefully into a seat next to him.

"Hi," Ayomi's voice sang out. Her amber-colored eyes bore directly into Kieran's.

"I'm Kieran," he said somewhat nervously, extending his hand. She giggled, but returned the gesture.

"That really is an odd human custom," Ayomi said.

"So I've been told," Kieran replied.

Tersha clapped his hands and called out another reading assignment. Several older Sunfires grumbled.

"When is Master Hartlan coming back?" one boy called out.

"He has not made me aware of his plans," Tersha said diplomatically. "Until Master Hartlan returns, he wishes for everyone to refresh their memories on subjects that often get neglected. Besides, this time of learning is very beneficial to our newest members."

The rustling of pages sounded loud in the otherwise silent room. Kieran flipped his book open and turned to a chapter titled "The First Founders." He started to read, but after a moment the words all seemed to blur together.

"Is class always so full of reading?" Ayomi whispered to Kieran.

"So far that's all we've done since I've been here."

"Would you want to read it together?"

"Sure," Kieran said. Ayomi brushed her hair over her shoulders and pulled her chair close. She leaned over his book and began reading aloud softly.

"In the early days of the age of Order, three mages of exemplary prowess came together to create a haven of learning and growth for young mages of all kind: Mitsala of Fierune, Tynavail of Odesia, and Frell of Lodlan. Each brought their own unique gifts. Frell the outgoing Alderan used his love of the earth and all its beauty to enrich the grounds and landscape around the palace. Frell founded Clan Terra, and at the side of the early students, raised stone to create the Academy's castle."

"Tynavail of Odesia, a calm and gentle Veshtu, brought his love of the water and its quietness. He came to lead Clan Aqua. With a quiet and caring nature, he gained the loyalty of students of all races."

"For the founding of Clan Ignis came stately Mitsala the Sombrayn. Her tenacious nature made her a force to be reckoned with, though her kind and noble heart kept her grounded. All three Founders gave immensely of their time and gifts to help establish the Academy of today's age. Exhibits of relics and tools they used can still be found today in the Hall of Founders."

As Ayomi finished reading, a thought sprang to Kieran's mind. He recalled High Seat Elrayan mentioning damage done to the Hall of the Founders at his trial. He hurriedly grabbed his book and rose from his chair.

"I'm sorry, but I've got to go!" Kieran mumbled the apology to Ayomi. He sprang for the door.

Chapter Fourteen
A Painful Lesson

"Tell me everything again."

"You've got to be kidding me!" Kieran declared. "I've already gone over it twice!"

"Then go over it a third. I need to hear every detail."

Kieran sighed but recounted the recent events to Luri. The two were walking about the grounds near Lake Ayhona. He told her of his conversation with Akiri about the incident in Tarmuth, of the interaction between Master Kaya and Caydn, and about what he learned of the Founders.

"I wonder what sort of objects they would have left behind," Kieran pondered.

"There are many stories," Luri stated. "However, it's hard to separate which are true and which are myth."

"I still wonder what that was on Master Hartlan's desk," Kieran stepped onto the path into Whisperwell Woods.

"I don't believe it would be one of the Founder's items."

"Why not?"

"Well, first of all," Luri began dramatically. "The Founders were very powerful mages. Any items they left behind would be full of strong magical energy. That's not the sort of thing someone would just leave lying around."

"Second, it sounds familiar," Luri continued. "Like something I've read about or seen. Can you describe it again, please?"

"It was small, really red, and kinda curved."

Luri scrunched her forehead. "I just can't seem to recall it."

Their footsteps were muffled on the dry dirt path. They could hear twigs snapping as small animals moved throughout the woods.

"Are you sure you feel up to a long walk?" Kieran asked his friend. "We can turn back if you need to rest. You did just get released by Master Rellus."

"I'm fine," Luri assured Kieran. "Besides, it feels good to be outside. Sometimes the castle can feel so... stuffy."

"Tell me about it," Kieran laughed. "What with all those dusty books everywhere!"

Luri shot him a look of fake annoyance at his joke. The two continued down the path deeper in the forest. It should have been cool in the shade of the thick trees; however, Kieran noticed that he was sweating.

"Something's not right," Akiri said fearfully to Kieran.

What is it? Kieran asked his magic. Akiri didn't respond. Kieran noticed that the sounds of the surrounding forest had all fallen silent. No birds sang. No animals played in the underbrush. Even the gentle breeze had stopped.

Luri seemed to notice it too. She hastily grabbed Kieran's hand.

"Kieran!" Luri whispered frantically. "We need to get out of here!"

Before either of them could move, the entire forest seemed to grow dark. Luri clapped her hand over her mouth and stifled a scream. She buried her face in Kieran's chest.

"Look up!" Akiri yelled to Kieran. He cocked his head back and tried to peer through the thick branches overhead.

Kieran would have yelled if he could have moved. It felt as if all the breath had left his lungs. He could make out the form of a massive, winged beast passing overhead. It was hard to tell much about its appearance, other than how large and dark-colored it was. The enormous creature let out an earth-shattering roar.

Kieran gripped Luri tighter and closed his eyes. *There's nothing I can do!* he thought desperately. *We're going to...*

"No!" Akiri commanded. "Stay still. It seems to be leaving."

Kieran waited for what felt like an eternity. He held Luri so firmly that he wondered if he was crushing her. After a moment, the woods seemed to return to normal. The sun shone through the branches once again and the noises of the forest sprang back to life.

Kieran released his grip on Luri and the two stared in silence. He could hear Luri's rapid breathing and watched as her eyes darted frantically around the forest. Her gaze landed on something on the ground before them.

"K-K-Kieran..." her voice stammered. "Is this what you saw on Hartlan's desk?"

Kieran bent down and picked up a small ruby object. It felt warm and smooth against his palm. It pulsed with magic, and Kieran could sense that it had also piqued Akiri's interest.

"Yes," he said, rubbing his fingers across its surface. "But what is it?"

Luri worked up the courage to speak. "That... that is a... dragon scale!"

"Cool!" Kieran exclaimed, tossing it up in the air and catching it. Luri jumped.

"Don't do that, Kieran! Dragons are powerful creatures. Even their scales hold enormous magical energy! You need to be careful!"

Kieran held the scale delicately. "So that means that creature we just saw was a real dragon!"

"Of course it was a *real* dragon, Kieran! It wasn't an illusion!" Luri shouted, bordering on hysterics. "With a dragon around, we need to get back to the Academy! We need to inform..."

Suddenly, Luri stopped in her tracks. She motioned to a figure coming down the path. Kieran recognized the white and scarlet robes.

"Flamemaster Caydn," Kieran mouthed to Luri. He swiftly stuck the dragon scale in his pocket.

Caydn approached the two friends with a somewhat worried expression on his face.

"Are you two unharmed?" Caydn was tense and scanned the woods around them.

"We're fine," Kieran replied stiffly. "The dragon didn't eat us."

Luri jabbed him hard in the ribs. Caydn looked at Kieran disapprovingly.

"An encounter with a dragon is nothing to scoff at, young mage," Caydn scolded. "You are both lucky to be alive."

"I don't think it noticed us, sir," Luri piped up. "It was flying pretty high overhead."

"What's a dragon doing out here, anyway?" Kieran asked.

"I do not know," Caydn said somberly. "It would appear this dragon has not been registered with the Order."

"The Order keeps a record of each dragon born," Luri explained to Kieran, noting his confused expression. "It is their way to keep track of where the dragons are."

"Precisely," Caydn agreed. "Now, we should make our way back to the Academy. I will escort you in case the dragon should return."

Kieran locked eyes with Caydn for a moment. He sensed there was more Caydn wished to say, but the Flamemaster stayed silent.

There's something odd about him, Akiri. Kieran thought as he and Luri fell in stride with Caydn.

As they walked, Kieran stuck his hand in his pocket and started fidgeting with the dragon scale. He grasped it tightly in his first and felt the heat against his skin.

"Wait, Kieran!" Akiri warned, but it was too late. The magical energy within the scale released and fire erupted in Kieran's pocket. He howled in pain and pulled his blistered hand out. The air stung his tender skin.

"Kieran!" Luri screeched as she spied his burnt hand.

The pain was nearly unbearable. Kieran carefully supported his injured hand, unsure of what to do.

"Come, young mage. We must get you to a healer," Caydn said.

"I can help!" Luri spoke up. She pulled some items from a small pouch at her waist. Caydn helped Kieran sit down on the ground as Luri organized her supplies. First, she took the stopper from a pale pink bottle. She gave Kieran a sympathetic look.

"I'm sorry, Kieran, this will sting, but I need to clean the burn."

As the liquid touched his skin, Kieran thought he might pass out from the pain. Luri quickly and gingerly placed her hands around his injured one. Kieran felt a cool, soothing sensation as Luri tapped into her healing ability. She held his hand for several minutes and Kieran felt the pain slowly recede to a faint tingling sensation. Finally, she let go of his hand.

Kieran held up his previously burnt hand that was miraculously no longer injured. The skin looked slightly pink and tender, but Kieran didn't feel any pain at all.

"That's incredible, Luri!" Kieran said with amazement. "Thanks!"

"You have quite the talent," Caydn praised. Luri blushed.

Caydn helped Kieran back to his feet and pointed himself back in the direction of the Academy.

"Now, young mages, if we can avoid any more incidences, we need to return to the castle."

Chapter Fifteen
The Dragon's Secret

Wilders. Ancient magical artifacts. Dragons. This place sure is a lot more interesting than Tarmuth!

"And dangerous," Akiri reminded Kieran. He paced around his room obsessing over the encounter in Whisperwell Woods. Luri had gone to lie down when they returned, but Kieran couldn't calm his racing mind. He flexed his hand, still amazed at how quickly Luri had healed it with magic.

I can't believe we saw a real dragon, Akiri! I never knew they lived so close!

"They can roost almost anywhere," Akiri explained. "However, most prefer to stay hidden. I would expect this one has a reason to stay nearby."

What sort of reason?

"I'm not sure," Akiri responded. "Perhaps if we found its roost, we could find some answers."

Well, it can't be too close to the castle. A dragon would not go unnoticed for long.

"I expect it roosts in the mountains," Akiri replied. "The mountain passes are dangerous, though. It would not do well to traverse them alone."

Kieran thought for a moment. Luri would never approve of searching after a dragon's roost. It would have to be someone else…

Ah! I know exactly who could help guide me to Mount Ulrah!

* * * * * *

Kieran struggled to breathe in the thin mountain air. His teeth chattered in the frosty fog. *Maybe this wasn't the best idea!*

"Come on, Kieran!" Shivyn's adventurous voice called out. "Just a bit farther!"

Don't look down! Don't look down! Kieran chanted. He reached his right hand out for a handhold. His gloved fingers slipped, and he cried out.

I'm going to die!

The panic passed and Kieran realized he still had firm footing and a strong grip with his left hand. Shivyn laughed up ahead.

"Come on, Sunfire! Show me some grit! Isn't that the quality of your Clan!"

Kieran summoned his courage and pushed on. Inch by inch, he scaled the rocky cliff. Reaching the top, Kieran flung himself to the ground and exhaled.

"What a rush!" he chuckled after a moment. "This is amazing, Shivyn!"

Shivyn smiled back at him. "Yeah, though Lulu hates that I do it. She's not going to be thrilled with you either."

"Well, I hadn't exactly planned to tell her."

"Ah," Shivyn gave a sly wink. "Always my policy."

Kieran looked below at the Academy. It seemed

so small from such a height. The Clan flags were just tiny ripples of color as the wind tossed them about. The students were like tiny beetles scurrying to and from their classes. Shivyn plopped down beside Kieran and dangled his legs over the edge.

"So what's the real reason we're up here, Kieran?"

"I just wanted to see the Academy from here," Kieran lied.

Shivyn looked at Kieran suspiciously, but shrugged it off.

"Okay then, now that you've seen the view, do you want to climb higher?" Shivyn motioned to a path leading further into the mountains.

Kieran grimaced. *Man, I hate heights! But I've got to find out if this dragon is roosting around the Academy.*

"Sure. Lead on, Shivyn."

Shivyn took off with a bounce and trekked onward. Kieran pushed back his fear and chased after him.

They hiked for hours. The early dawn of their departure gave way into mid-afternoon. Kieran grew nervous.

"Shivyn," Kieran panted. "Maybe it's time we turn back. We don't want to be up here at dark."

"We'll turn back when you find what you're looking for."

As Kieran opened his mouth to protest, Shivyn turned around with a sly grin.

"You're not fooling me, Sunfire. Now, tell me what you're looking for."

Kieran's mind raced as he tried to think of something to tell Shivyn. Before he could stop himself, Kieran blurted out.

"I'm looking for a dragon's roost."

Shivyn looked at Kieran with pure astonishment. He quickly composed himself and let out a soft laugh.

"Well, that sounds easy enough," Shivyn said, running his hand through his light hair. "Come on, let's get on with it."

"Wait! You mean you believe me, just like that?"

Shivyn looked straight into Kieran's face. "Are you lying to me, Kieran?"

"Of course not!"

"Then I believe you." Shivyn turned back to the trail. He looked at Kieran once more. "Anyone that makes you prove your word doubts you from the beginning."

*   *   *   *   *   *

Kieran's legs burned with a fire he'd never felt before, and not of magical origins. *I won't even be able to walk tomorrow!* Kieran lamented.

The mountainside was steep and overgrown with thick vegetation. Kieran knew they must be drawing close to the dragon's roost because the ground was littered with stray dragon scales. Kieran pulled a scrap piece of cloth from his pocket and carefully picked one up.

"Kieran!" Akiri scolded. "Didn't your incident

yesterday teach you anything?"

I know to be more careful this time, Kieran replied. *But you never know when a dragon scale could come in handy.* He wrapped the cloth around the scale and placed it in his pocket, careful to not touch it.

Kieran pressed on after Shivyn. They had nearly reached the top of the tallest peak when Shivyn called out.

Kieran pushed his aching legs onward and reached a flat clearing where Shivyn stood frozen. The grass was all pressed flat and a pile of twigs created a small border.

"A nest!" Kieran exclaimed.

"And it's not empty," Shivyn marveled, pointing to something nestled in the center.

Kieran leaned over the side of the massive nest to make it out more clearly. It was larger than Kieran's head and covered in what looked like scales. It was a rich, ebony-red color, and the sun glinted off of it.

"A dragon egg!" Kieran exclaimed. He looked over to Shivyn who was eyeing the egg with an almost hungry look in his eye.

"Shivyn... are you okay?" Kieran felt uneasy.

"Do you know what this means, Kieran?" Shivyn asked with a manic glee. "A dragon has not been born in Peria for hundreds of years. Their kind has been laying dormant in our lands. This egg is proof of the changing tide!"

Kieran watched Shivyn closely, worried. *He's not acting right.*

"Dragons and their eggs emanate great power," Akiri cautioned. "You and your friend need to leave this place."

Kieran agreed with Akiri and grabbed Shivyn by the arm. "We need to get out of here!"

Shivyn didn't respond. He continued to eye the egg as if in a trance. He slowly stretched out his hand toward it.

"No!" Kieran yelled, pulling Shivyn back. "Don't touch it, Shivyn!"

Just before Shivyn's fingers grazed the egg, a loud, threatening roar startled both boys. Shivyn jolted from his trance, looking terrified.

"The mother is coming! Come on, Shivyn, we have to get out of here!"

Another shriek resonated through the mountains. Shivyn bolted from the nest without pausing for Kieran.

"Wait!" Kieran yelled, taking off after him.

Both boys stumbled back down the mountain path. The rocks were loose and Kieran nearly tripped multiple times, though something seemed to help hold him steady as he continued to run.

A pulse of heat, undoubtedly from the dragon, hit Kieran as he ran. Akiri helped him field the magical pulse. Its warmth seemed to settle inside Kieran, rather than injure him.

"Don't pause!" Akiri urged. "Flame dragons can breathe fire, and I'm not sure I could guard against it!"

Noted, Kieran thought, not that he needed any further reason to run.

The angry cries of the dragon continued to echo as Kieran and Shivyn neared the cliff edge. Both boys hastily hoisted themselves over the side and began climbing down.

As they were about halfway down the cliff face, the dragon reappeared above them. Kieran watched in horror as she seemed to free fall toward them. She tucked her massive wings against her sides and darted past them. Kieran gripped the rock face as tightly as he could, his muscles quivering in protest.

The dragon pulled out of her dive just before careening into the ground and flew off, presumably back toward her nest. Kieran held his breath as he watched her fade into the distance. When he was satisfied that she wasn't coming back, Kieran looked below to Shivyn. Suddenly, Kieran's heart stopped.

Rather than being just below Kieran on the cliff face, Shivyn was lying unmoving on the ground.

Chapter Sixteen
The Last Piece

"Kieran! Kieran? Are you all right?"

"I'm fine," Kieran mumbled, trying to make sense of his surroundings. Luri stood beside him looking worried. Kieran realized he was sitting on a bed with green sheets.

"How did I wind up in the recovery wing?" Kieran tried to stand. Luri gently eased him back onto the bed.

"You're in shock, Kieran. You need to rest here." Luri's voice was kind and gentle.

"What happened?" Kieran asked her, unable to piece it all together.

"There was an accident," Luri said softly. "You and Shivyn were climbing up to Mount Ulrah and Shivyn fell." Tears sprang to her eyes.

"No," Kieran closed his eyes. "Don't tell me Shivyn is..."

"Oh! No, no! Shivyn's alive!" Luri hugged Kieran. "And I have you to thank. If he had been alone, well, I don't want to think about what would have happened. Don't you remember running for help?"

Kieran thought back. He could remember stumbling upon the dragon's nest and being chased back to the cliff. He shuddered at the memory of seeing Shivyn lying on the ground below.

"I remember," Kieran whispered. "I was afraid I wouldn't reach help in time."

"But you did! Master Rellus was able to get to Shivyn quickly. He hit his head pretty hard and can't remember some things, but he's going to be okay."

Kieran stayed quiet, still mulling the events over in his head. *Should I tell Luri about the egg?*

"You need to forget about the dragon for now," Akiri warned. "Dragons have led to the fall of many mages. Their power is too great. You saw how it affected Shivyn."

I know, Akiri, but Luri's my friend. She'd want to know about what happened.

Before Kieran could tell Luri about what had really happened on Mount Ulrah, Master Rellus came into the room.

"Luri, your brother is awake."

"Ah!" Luri cried excitedly. She leapt to her feet then suddenly paused and looked back at Kieran.

"Will you be all right by yourself, Kieran?"

"Yeah, I'm fine," he assured her. "Go see your brother."

With a gentle smile and a nod to Kieran, Luri followed Master Rellus. A Moonglow student came by and gave Kieran a final check before determining he could leave the recovery wing. Kieran happily obliged.

He walked back through the castle and headed for the door. His thoughts still swirled viciously in his head.

Something is going on, Akiri. All of this has to mean something! Tarmuth... the dragon scale... the Hall of the Founders... the stolen object... the dragon... the egg... I just can't figure it out!

"Kieran?"

Kieran jumped at the sound of a soft voice. He looked up to see Ayomi standing nearby, watching him curiously.

"Are you all right? I heard there was an accident at Mount Ulrah."

"I'm fine," Kieran said hastily, tiring of repeating the phrase.

Ayomi's cheeks turned red and Kieran immediately felt rotten for having been rude.

"I'm sorry, Ayomi. It's just been a rough day."

Ayomi tucked her long hair behind her ear. "Would you like to go for a walk?"

Kieran chuckled. "I think I've had enough walks lately. How about we just sit for a while?"

Ayomi smiled. "That sounds nice, too."

Kieran and Ayomi sat down beneath a large tree. White buds were forming on its twisting branches. They sat for a while before Ayomi broke the silence.

"You lived in Tarmuth before you came to the Academy, correct?" Ayomi asked.

"Yeah," Kieran replied.

"What did your parents do?"

"I don't know. I never met them."

Ayomi blushed again. "I'm so sorry, I didn't mean..."

"It's all right," Kieran assured her. "It's odd, I guess. When you grow up without something, it's kinda hard to miss it."

"I guess that's true," Ayomi said thoughtfully. "My family lives in a small village on the outskirts, but my father works in the city."

"What does your father do?"

"He's a historian at the Hall of the Founders."

Kieran's heart skipped a beat. *Maybe I can find the missing piece...*

"I bet he's been busy," Kieran said, trying to reign in his excitement. "What with the attack in Tarmuth and all."

"Yes," Ayomi replied unassumingly. "The Hall of the Founders was badly damaged."

Kieran's interest was piqued. "I heard rumors that something was taken as well."

Ayomi gave Kieran a suspicious glance. "Yes..." she said slowly. "Though details of that haven't been shared from the Order."

"But I bet your father knows what was taken," Kieran prodded. When Ayomi didn't answer, Kieran changed his approach.

"It's just... I don't remember much from that night in Tarmuth, but it feels important. Maybe if I knew more of what happened, my memories might resurface."

Ayomi was quiet. She took in a deep breath and finally spoke.

"You mustn't tell anyone what I'm about to tell you."

"Of course not," Kieran said sincerely, looking directly into Ayomi's eyes. "You have my word."

Ayomi leaned in. "Someone broke into Ignis Hall and stole Mitsala's Amulet."

"What's that?"

"Mitsala's Amulet is an ancient relic forged by powerful flame magic. It allows the wearer to absorb outside sources of fire magic and pull them in as their own."

"That sounds... complicated," Kieran said.

Ayomi smiled. "Imagine you were facing a powerful mage more strongly gifted than you in fire magic. His ability could easily overpower your own. But if you were wearing Mitsala's Amulet, you could draw in that power and combine it with your own, doubling your power."

"And Mitsala's Amulet can also affect natural sources of magic such as Heatstone," Ayomi continued. "So as you can see, a person wearing the amulet could build magic from many various sources."

"That's crazy!" Kieran exclaimed.

"Mitsala is one of my favorite mages to study," Ayomi said. "Her story is fascinating! She was such a calm and intelligent Founder, yet she had incredible power and strength. There are many legends and stories about her accomplishments."

"Like what?" Kieran asked, genuinely curious.

"Some people believe that she was a Midling."

A Midling! Kieran thought excitedly. *Could a Founder of the Academy really have been a Midling?*

"It's also rumored that Mitsala created a place within the Academy filled with immense fire magic," Ayomi said excitedly. "It's called the Ignis Lair."

That's it! Kieran thought excitedly.

"Thanks, Ayomi," Kieran blurted, rising from the ground.

"Where are you going, Kieran? Have you remembered something?"

"Yes," he lied. "I need to go, but you've really helped!"

*   *   *   *   *   *

"This is bad."

Kieran watched as Luri paced in his room. He had just told her about his conversation with Ayomi.

"If Hartlan stole Mitsala's Amulet, and has a flame dragon scale, he could open the lair of Ignis."

"I still don't understand why he would do it," Kieran said.

"There must be something down there that Hartlan wants."

"Like what?"

"Something that would give him the power to challenge the Order, I suppose," Luri guessed. "We need to tell someone."

"Well, we can't go to the Order. They all listen to Caydn and he was way too close to Hartlan at my trial. I think they're working together."

"There must be someone," Luri continued pacing. "Ah! I know! Master Kovesh's family is very prominent in the Order, and as the head of Clan Ignis, he'd know about the Lair. Perhaps he would know what Hartlan is after."

"You really think it's a good idea to tell Master Kovesh about this?"

Luri stopped pacing. "Kieran, I don't think we have much of a choice. If Master Hartlan opens the Ignis Lair, who knows what could happen here. He needs to be stopped."

Luri and Kieran made their way discreetly to Master Kovesh's classroom. Luri kept giving Kieran gentle nudges to hurry.

I'm not sure about this, Akiri, Kieran said. *Something just doesn't add up.*

"Trust your instincts, Kieran," Akiri replied. "Stay alert and vigilant."

Kieran took heed of Akiri's words, but couldn't find enough reason to not follow Luri to Master Kovesh. They wound their way down the long corridors with the flaming torches. As they approached the classroom, they found the door slightly ajar.

"Master Kovesh doesn't have a class at this time of day," Luri stated. "He's probably in his office."

The two went through the door into the classroom. It felt empty and hollow with no students trying to wield flame within it. An odd quietness hung in the air.

"Something's not right here, Luri."

Luri walked further into the room toward a door at the back.

"Master Kovesh?" she called out softly, then

louder. "Master Kovesh? Are you here?"

Kieran motioned for Luri to get behind him. Slowly, he approached the door to Kovesh's office and pushed it open.

Just as the room before it, the office sat empty. A large desk occupied most of the space in the room. It was extremely neat and tidy, very unlike the desk in Master Hartlan's office.

The air in the room was warm, and Kieran could easily feel the remnants of heat. He looked around and noticed scorch marks on the wall behind the desk.

"Look, Luri!"

Luri bent down and brushed her fingertips across the marks. "What do you think happened in here, Kieran?"

"I don't know, but it doesn't look good."

"What if Master Hartlan forced Master Kovesh to take him to the Ignis Lair?" Luri asked fearfully.

"But where is the lair?" Kieran wondered.

Suddenly, a warmth arose in Kieran and he felt a strange sensation from Akiri.

"I've been here before," Akiri stated plainly.

Okay, Kieran began. *Is the entrance to the Ignis lair here?*

"Yes."

Kieran grew excited. "Luri, Akiri can help us find the entrance!"

"That's great, Kieran, but how?"

Kieran closed his eyes. *Let me help you this time, Akiri.*

He blocked out the world around him and tried to focus only on the presence he had come to know. He could tell Akiri was thinking very hard, trying to remember flickers from his past. Kieran envisioned the line of magic like he had been practicing and tried to slow down its rhythm. It started to pulse in time to the rhythm of Akiri's.

"There!" Akiri said finally. He directed Kieran's gaze to an unassuming place on the wall.

What's there? Kieran asked curiously.

"The entrance to the Ignis Lair is there. Kieran, pull out the dragon scale."

Kieran did as Akiri told. He reached into his pocket and pulled out the scale, carefully unwrapping it from the cloth. Immediately the draw of its power started to entice Kieran.

Luri gasped. "Kieran! When did you..?"

"Not now," Kieran said, not wanting to go into the real reason he and Shivyn had gone to the mountain.

Akiri helped Kieran slowly draw flame magic from the scale. Rippling crimson fire encircled Kieran. Luri dashed to the side of the room shielding her eyes.

As Kieran raised his hand, a glowing circle appeared on the wall before him. It was comprised of runic symbols that Kieran didn't understand. However, he felt Akiri's urge to place his hand in the center.

The flames around Kieran flared for a moment and then vanished. With a loud jolt, the stone wall receded a few inches and abruptly dropped to the floor, leaving an opening large enough for Kieran and Luri to walk through. Luri stepped closer to Kieran and tugged at his sleeve.

"We shouldn't go down there alone," she whispered.

"You can stay," Kieran said. "But I'm going to find out what's going on."

"I'm not going to let you go by yourself!" Luri said defiantly. She scanned Kovesh's office and found an unlit torch. She passed it to Kieran who found he had no trouble conjuring a flame to light it. Kieran raised it above his head, illuminating the long tunnel in front of them.

"Let's go."

Chapter Seventeen
Into the Unknown

Kieran had no idea what to expect as he and Luri entered the Ignis Lair. The corridor they stepped into was dark as night past the glow of the torch. Kieran moved the light steadily to illuminate the walls. They were a smooth, inky black stone with ruby and gold flecks throughout.

Akiri urged Kieran to reach out and touch the wall. As he did, a warmth drew to the surface. Kieran pulled back his hand to see a glowing imprint where his palm had been. It slowly faded back to black.

"Wow! Luri, did you see that?"

"I did," Luri replied curtly. "But we do not have time to play with stone. We need to hurry and find Master Kovesh. If he was attacked by Master Hartlan, he could be in very real danger."

Kieran traced his fingertips across the stone lightly as he walked further into the lair. Streaks of light were left behind in his wake.

What is this stuff? Kieran asked Akiri.

"That is Heatstone," Akiri answered. "It can store heat energy inside it."

Kieran placed his hand on it again. He pulled in the warmth from the stone.

This is amazing! Kieran thought.

The corridor began to slope downward and twist and turn. Kieran moved the torch closer to the wall, drawing out the energy of the stone as he passed. The corridor was filled with more fleeting light. At each new turn, Kieran stopped and peered around, but was not met with anyone.

"It's boiling down here," Luri complained. She was panting and dripping with sweat.

Kieran felt the heat, but he drew it into himself so that it invigorated rather than drained him.

She doesn't look good, Kieran said to Akiri.

"Those that aren't flame attuned will find the temperatures of this area too hot to handle," Akiri replied.

"Luri," Kieran urged. "I think you should turn back."

"I won't leave you alone down here, Kieran." Her tone was resolute.

The echoes of their footsteps changed pitch as they walked.

"We must be approaching an open chamber," Luri whispered.

"Be on guard," Akiri advised.

Kieran's heart raced as they continued on.

Thud. Thud. Thud.

Kieran could no longer tell if it was the sound of his heartbeat or his footsteps. The darkness finally gave way to a bright, open chamber.

High, molded stone ceilings swept overhead. The chamber had been ornately crafted and shaped. More of the Heatstone filled the room and the glow of fiery orbs danced at the ceiling.

In sharp contrast to the heat sources, a shallow chasm ran through the floor. Water gently trickled through it.

Kieran bent down and placed his hand in the water.

"It's cold!" he marveled.

Luri pointed to glowing symbols etched into the inside of the chasm. "Runes keep the water cool."

The chasm was narrow enough that Kieran and Luri could step across it with wide steps.

As soon as Kieran's foot touched down on the other side, it was like an overpowering wave of heat hit him. The shock of it sent Kieran to his knees. He heard Akiri and Luri calling out to him, but his vision started to fade to black.

"Stay strong, Kieran!" Akiri called out. Kieran pushed against the feeling and forced himself back to his feet.

A slow clap came from behind Luri and Kieran, making them jump.

"Well, done, young mage, you've come far since your evaluation test. That sort of magical power would have knocked you flat before."

Kieran whipped around expecting to see Master Hartlan, but was confused to find Master Kovesh standing tall.

"What are you doing here?" Kieran asked incredulously.

"A question more befitting for the two of you," Kovesh sneered. He began walking toward Kieran and Luri. Kieran noticed a jeweled necklace around Kovesh's neck.

"Mitsala's Amulet!" Kieran cried. "But why do you have it?"

"You are rather thick, aren't you, boy? Oh well, I'll indulge you this once, it's not like it will matter, anyway."

Kovesh walked directly in front of Kieran and raised his arms. "This!" Kovesh began, "is the Ignis Lair, designed by the founder of Ignis, the illustrious Mitsala!"

He continued. "Mitsala was a wise and powerful mage in her time. She had more prowess with the flame artes in her youth than most can wish to gain in a lifetime!"

"She, along with the other founders Tynavail and Frell, came up with the idea to have dens of powerful magic. Now these dens, or lairs as they've come to be known, were too powerful for those of normal status to enter. I mean, look at your friend."

Kieran looked at Luri who had nearly collapsed on the ground. He started toward her, but a crackling snap of lightning struck the ground between them.

"No, no, young mage, I won't have you being distracted from my tale," Kovesh chided. "Now, only those of true ability can withstand the power that flows within this chamber. You have surprised me, young fire wielder, but I had sensed that you were different all along."

"Why did you do this, Kovesh?" Kieran yelled. "I don't understand!"

"Naive, young mage," Kovesh jeered. "You know so little of this world. The Founders were mages of a different era, an era before the rise of the Order. The Order has stifled the magic that exists in this world. We are left with mere scraps of what is truly available for the taking! The Order has made us weak! But you will see, young mage, that will not be so for much longer!"

Kovesh started walking toward the center of the chamber where a tall stone altar stood. A dozen spiral steps led up to the ornate altar. Kovesh glided up the steps to the top. Kieran watched as Kovesh again raised his arms, this time pulling magical energy from the room toward him.

"Shield Luri from him!" Akiri called out.

Kieran leapt to Luri's side where she lay breathing heavily, almost lifeless. He stooped over her, trying to block her from Master Kovesh.

"We've got the get out of here!" Kieran urged. "Let me help you up!"

Luri tried to stand, but couldn't. "Just go, Kieran! You've got to get out of here!"

"Not without you!"

Kieran tried again to pull Luri to her feet, but feared he would hurt her. Frustrated, he turned his gaze back to Master Kovesh. He still stood at the altar drawing in the magical energy from around him. The fiery orbs at the ceiling looked much smaller now as he drained them of their energy.

I can't let him do this! Kieran said to Akiri. *Tell me what to do!*

"I'm afraid he's too powerful already," Akiri warned. "I cannot compete with the magic he has gathered with the Amulet!"

I have to do something!

Kieran rose from his place at Luri's side and ran toward the center of the room. Kovesh seemed almost in a trance as he continued pulling in magical energy. The amulet glowed brightly at his chest.

Help me, Akiri! Kieran pleaded as he mustered up the strength to summon magic. He felt the ebb and flow: his line and Akiri's. He eased his breathing in line with the pulse, envisioning an inner flame.

Flames came forth from Kieran's palms and hovered above them. Kieran let out a yell and shot the fire from his hands towards Kovesh.

The flames seemed to hit an invisible barrier around Kovesh and immediately dissipate. Kovesh took notice of the hit, though he was unharmed. He turned his gaze back to Kieran.

"Run!" Akiri yelled. Kieran felt the swell of magic in the room, but couldn't move. An enormous fireball came careening toward Kieran.

Instinctively, Kieran put his hands up, knowing that he could do nothing to stop the hit. Before the fire made contact, Kieran heard a loud hiss and felt steam on his face.

Luri stood near Kieran, breathing heavily with her right hand outstretched. She had drawn from the water in the chasm and used it to extinguish the fireball. The exertion seemed to be too much for her, though, and she doubled over.

"Come on, Luri!" Kieran yelled, draping her arm around his shoulders. "Let's get out of here!"

"You're not going anywhere!" Kovesh yelled out maniacally. With a sweep of his hand, flames sprang up blocking the entrance to the lair. Kieran took a step backward.

We're trapped!

Chapter Eighteen
Fateful Flames

Kieran felt Luri quivering with fear as he supported her weight. He was afraid to set her back on the floor, but also knew that he couldn't wield at all while he tried to keep her steady.

From the look of her, Luri had nothing more to give, either. Her skin was no longer sweaty but was unnaturally dry. Her lips were pale and cracked.

"She won't survive this heat much longer," Akiri said. "She's not progressed enough in the water artes to adequately shield herself from the power Kovesh has released."

What do I do? Kieran wondered frantically.

Kovesh was still at the altar. After Kieran's interruption, Kovesh had turned his attention back to drawing from the power of the lair.

"STOOOOOOPPPPP!" a voice boomed.

The flames in the entrance immediately disappeared as someone rushed into the room. His hands were raised, and he brought forth a fiery whip that he cracked at Kovesh.

"Master Hartlan!" Kieran cried out, realizing who had come. Hartlan ignored Kieran and Luri and charged at Kovesh. Kovesh grinned wickedly.

"Ah, I expected you, Hartlan!" Kovesh sneered. "Killing you here will save me a lot of trouble later!"

Rather than respond with words, Master Hartlan aimed the whip at Kovesh's face. Kovesh threw up his hands and pushed out with a magical pulse, sending the whip careening to the floor.

Hartlan's feet shifted, and he pulled his hands in front of his chest. Magical energy gathered between his palms and he formed a compact fireball. With a yell, Hartlan lobbed it at Kovesh.

Kovesh dodged and sent back his own fireball twice the size of Hartlan's. It narrowly missed its mark and hit the stone with a boom that sent echoes throughout the chamber.

Luri screamed as pieces of rock came falling down near them. Kieran pulled her out of the way just in time.

"You should realize you're no longer a match for me!" Kovesh boasted. "I have the true power of Ignis at my disposal!"

Kovesh's body became encircled with flames. The fire built and built before Kovesh released it toward Kieran, Luri, and Hartlan.

This is it! We're going to die! Kieran thought hopelessly.

A wall of water sprang up shielding them from Kovesh's attack. Kieran still held on to Luri, who was limp at his side.

Who did that? Kieran asked Akiri. Akiri nudged Kieran's gaze toward Master Hartlan. Hartlan's hands were stretched out in front of him, pushing the wall of water higher and higher to block the flames. He threw his arms to the side, sending the water like a torrential wave directly at Kovesh. It hit him directly, extinguishing the fire surrounding his body.

"You may harness the power of Ignis," Hartlan's voice boomed. "But you were foolish to underestimate my power, Kovesh!"

Kovesh wore a bewildered expression on his face. He scrambled back to his feet.

"You'll regret this!" Kovesh bellowed at Hartlan. He turned toward an exit at the far side of the chamber and took off. Hartlan turned to Kieran and Luri. He scooped Luri into his arms.

"We must get out of here, Kieran. Luri needs to see Master Rellus immediately."

"But what about Kovesh?" Kieran asked. "We can't just let him get away! He has Mitsala's Amulet!"

"We must leave before this cavern collapses," Hartlan warned sternly. He turned to leave.

I can't just let Kovesh get away! Kieran said to Akiri. *I've got to do something!*

Kieran looked at Master Hartlan's back for a moment, then turned and bolted after Kovesh. Master Hartlan whipped back around.

"Kieran! No!"

*　　　*　　　*　　　*　　　*　　　*

Kieran finally began to slow as the last echoes of Hartlan's voice faded. He was in another long corridor just like the one he and Luri had first come through. The walls here were also made of Heatstone.

The walls still held the glow of Kovesh's presence as he had passed through. Kieran continued on until he realized the path was sloping upward.

The sky soon appeared before Kieran as he emerged from the tunnel into the open air. He could hear faint sounds of the Academy in the distance, so he knew he couldn't be too far. The tunnel had opened at the base of the mountains.

He must be going for the dragon! Kieran thought.

Night had now fallen, making Kieran wonder how long they had been down in the Ignis Lair. The inky black sky was dotted with stars.

"I can help you sense for Kovesh's magic," Akiri offered. "Close your eyes and focus on the magic around you."

Kieran did as Akiri said. He tried to feel for the pulse of Kovesh's magic.

I can't find it! Kieran exclaimed, frustrated.

"Try once more," Akiri encouraged. Kieran reached out again, trying to fully block out his surroundings. He could feel a flicker of heat coming from his right.

There! Kieran exclaimed. He opened his eyes and took off in the direction of the heat. Kieran looked up to see Kovesh heading toward the mountain.

"We must be careful," Akiri warned. "Kovesh has absorbed an incredible amount of power."

Kieran stayed low and followed Kovesh. He tried to move silently, but his foot caught on the rocky ground and he stumbled.

"Oof!"

Kovesh jerked around toward Kieran, conjuring a large flame.

"Stupid boy! Following me will be the last mistake you ever make!"

Horror washed over Kieran as he watched the flames swirl about Kovesh. At Kovesh's direction, the flames wrapped around his body and formed into fiery wings, like those of a dragon.

"Goodbye, Kieran of Tarmuth!" Kovesh roared. The flames shot forward and hit Kieran squarely in the chest. He was entirely consumed by the flames.

"Kieran!" Akiri's voice called out.

The flames burned Kieran's skin, and he screamed out in agony.

Help me, Akiri! Kieran begged.

Just as Kieran thought it was all over, he felt Akiri connect with him once more. A sudden, soothing feeling washed over his body. Kieran's magic rose to the surface to combat the intensity of Kovesh's fire.

"Stand, Kieran!" Akiri commanded.

Kieran rose to his feet, still enshrouded in fire. He felt the urge to push it forward. Kieran gasped in awe when he saw it gain a form.

Conjured before Kieran was a large, fiery bird. It sparkled with glowing embers.

A phoenix! Kieran stared in amazement.

Kovesh looked at the phoenix with utter disbelief. He tried to overpower it with his own flames, but the phoenix seemed to absorb the fire.

"This is impossible!" Kovesh shouted with venom. "Only the most powerful of the ancient mages could conjure a phoenix!" He stepped closer to Kieran.

"Kieran!" a sudden voice called out. Caydn and several members of the Order rushed to Kieran's side.

Kovesh stepped back away from the members of the Order. A dark look crossed over his face.

"You will survive this encounter, boy, but don't expect to be so lucky in the future!"

Kovesh let out a loud clicking noise. It was met with a deafening roar from deeper in the mountains.

An enormous ruby dragon swooped down from the sky before Kovesh. Kovesh grabbed the scales on the beast's back and pulled himself astride it.

"We will meet again, and you will not find yourself so fortunate the next time!" Kovesh leaned forward sharply, and the dragon took off into the air. Caydn and the others shot magical sparks into the sky, but the dragon rose higher and higher until it was out of sight.

Kieran dropped to his knees. His head was spinning, and he felt like he would be sick. Akiri seemed taxed as well, and the conjured phoenix vanished.

Caydn's voice called out, but Kieran's vision faded to black.

Chapter Nineteen
The Midlings

.

Argh, my chest!

Kieran grabbed at his chest. It felt as if it were on fire. A gentle touch pushed Kieran's hand back down.

"I know it hurts, but you mustn't touch it," Master Rellus said calmly.

Kieran's vision cleared, and he found himself in the recovery wing. He looked down at his chest and noticed it was heavily bandaged.

"What..."

"You were injured by Master Kovesh," Master Rellus explained. "It's a miracle that you withstood his power as well as you did. Your burns are minor, but will take some time to fully heal."

"Luri!" Kieran exclaimed, looking around frantically.

"She is recovering, but will also be fine. Master Hartlan brought her to me quickly."

"Was anyone else hurt?" Kieran asked.

"Fortunately, no," Master Rellus replied. "Master Kovesh could have caused a great deal of harm."

Kieran still felt frustrated. *He got away!* He said to Akiri.

"I know," Akiri replied softly. "However, you

were able to keep him from harming anyone else."

"How long do I have to stay here?" Kieran asked Master Rellus.

A faint smile spread across Master Rellus' face. "A few days, perhaps. You will have plenty of visitors to keep you company, though."

Kieran gave Master Rellus a puzzled look as the teacher rose to his feet. He tipped his head toward the door. Master Hartlan had just stepped through it.

"Ah, Kieran. You're awake."

Hartlan walked up to Kieran and took a seat beside his bed. Master Rellus gave Hartlan a polite nod and walked away.

"You must have many questions, Kieran."

"Yeah, that's for sure," Kieran said. "For starters, what really happened in Tarmuth the night I was captured."

Hartlan took in a breath. "Kovesh was in Tarmuth the night you were accused. He broke into the Hall of Founders and stole Mitsala's Amulet."

"Why can't I remember much of that night?" Kieran asked.

"It would seem that you are very open to the magic of others," Hartlan explained. "When Kovesh attacked the Hall of the Founders to steal the Amulet, he set loose magical fires that you came into contact with. The magic he possessed came from a dark place not in alignment with the Order."

"So he's a Wilder then?"

"Yes," Hartlan continued. "Now, I feel we should

address your own abilities."

Kieran's stomach lurched.

"Few mages have been able to wield such powerful fire magic," Hartlan began. "Not since the time of Mitsala has anyone ever produced a phoenix."

"Is that bad?" Kieran asked worriedly.

"Not at all," Master Hartlan replied kindly. "I've sensed something in you since we met, and after the events in the Ignis lair, I now know what that something is."

"I'm a Midling," Kieran said before Hartlan could continue.

"Yes, but not just any Midling," Hartlan said. "Kieran, do you know why you could open the door to the Ignis Lair?"

"Because I had a dragon scale."

"Yes, but how did you know to use it?"

Kieran thought for a moment. "Akiri told me."

Hartlan smiled mysteriously. "Kieran, Akiri has been around a lot longer than you may realize. The magical presence that resides in a Midling is passed on from mage to mage throughout the passing of time. Akiri was able to aid you so much in the Ignis Lair because he was a part of its creation."

"So it's true that Mitsala was a Midling!" Kieran exclaimed. "So you mean Akiri was with one of the Founders?"

"Yes. Mitsala used Akiri's unique abilities when she created the amulet, abilities that he now passes to you."

"Like with the Moonstone and Heatstone," Kieran realized.

"Yes."

"So how do you know so much about my abilities?" Kieran asked.

"Because they are similar to my own," Hartlan replied.

Kieran thought for a moment. "You're a Midling too!" he realized. "That's how you could use water artes in the Ignis Lair!"

"Yes," Hartlan said with a nod. "Though my magic is limited in some areas. I could feel the presence of a Wilder at the Academy, but could not pinpoint the source."

"So if Kovesh stole the amulet from Tarmuth, why did he wait so long to open the Ignis Lair?"

"He had to learn how to gain access to it, I presume," Hartlan said. "Just as you did when you found the dragon scale."

"But you had a dragon scale! I saw it on your desk!"

"I did. It is my job as the leader of the Academy to investigate why a dragon would draw so near."

"Kovesh called it, didn't he?"

"Yes. He must have found a way to subdue it and gain its obedience. I expect the amulet was a great aid to him."

Kieran sat quiet for a moment. So many more questions continued to swirl in his head.

"What will happen now? Will the Order stay at

the Academy?"

"For a time," Hartlan said. "The Order will be on high alert since Kovesh's betrayal. There also exists a danger to the students as long as he remains at large. Until the Order brings him into custody, it is imperative to stay vigilant."

*   *   *   *   *   *

Three days passed slowly as Kieran recovered. Each day the healing students and Master Rellus came and changed Kieran's bandages.

"Your recovery is astounding!" Master Rellus said, discarding the bandages. "I've never seen a student recover from such a burn so quickly."

"Does that mean I can leave?" Kieran asked.

"Soon," Master Rellus chuckled. "You overexerted yourself significantly. Your body still needs time to recover. Once more night and I think you will be well enough to leave."

Kieran spent the next night in restless dreams. Though Kovesh was no longer at the Academy, something continued to bother Kieran, but he couldn't pinpoint what it was. He dreamed of dark, swirling figures. Kieran could not discern much more about them, but still awoke the next morning in a cold, nervous sweat.

Master Rellus released Kieran from the recovery wing come morning. Kieran quickly made his way to breakfast. The food on the healing wing was far healthier than Kieran preferred, and he longed for a sugary pastry.

Standing in the doorway of the dining hall were two beaming faces.

"Shivyn! Luri! You're both okay!"

"Thanks to you!" Luri ran up and hugged Kieran. "You were very brave!"

"How are you feeling, Shivyn?" Kieran asked. Shivyn still sported a bandage wrapped around his head. Luri stood very close to him, eyeing him.

"Never better!" Shivyn joked. "Though I still don't remember why we climbed Mount Ulrah in the first place."

"I just wanted to see it," Kieran lied. It felt odd to still hold secrets from Shivyn and Luri, but...

Wait a minute! Kieran alerted Akiri to his thoughts. *What about the dragon egg? Do you think Kovesh took it when he left?*

"Doubtful," Akiri replied. "He left in quite a hurry."

Then I wonder what will happen to it when it hatches.

Kieran's thoughts were interrupted by Luri pulling him into the dining hall to fix a plate. Kieran was delighted to see stacks of his favorite pastries. Luri gave him her customary disapproving glance, but it did nothing to deter Kieran from piling his plate high.

"There's Artemael," Luri whispered as she nudged Kieran. Kieran looked to the table where Artemael sat surrounded by somber Ignis students.

"He's still here?" Kieran asked.

"Well, he didn't do anything," Luri replied.

"Being related to Kovesh is offense enough," Kieran said bitterly.

"He's furious, you know," Luri warned Kieran. "Word has spread since your fight with Kovesh. It's all anyone is talking about. And there's something else…"

"What?" Kieran asked.

Luri looked anxious. "Kieran, your secret is out. Everyone knows you're a Midling."

It should have bothered Kieran, however, he felt at peace.

"That's okay," he said calmly. "I think attitudes about Midlings are about to change. I hear I'm in some powerful company."

Luri looked perplexed at Kieran's words, but soon a sudden hush fell over the room as Master Hartlan entered. Caydn stood at his side as Hartlan came before the students.

"Good students, I hope the day finds you well!" Hartlan called out cheerfully.

He was met with pleasant murmurs from most of the students. Artemael and his friends stayed broodingly silent.

"I'm sure curiosity is boiling at this point," Hartlan continued. "I feel it is time that you all come to learn the true nature of the events that have transpired in the last few days."

"First, it is with a heavy heart I must announce that Master Kovesh is no longer a teacher and ally of the Academy. His choices have led him down a path not in alignment with the values we hold dear."

"In his stead, the Academy will welcome a new Flamemaster, Master Vellavira, who will take over as head of Clan Ignis. Though she is currently traveling, I urge you all to welcome her warmly when she arrives."

"Next, the Order finds that the stability of the school is coming back into balance and feels they will have no need to maintain a continued presence here. However, they have left one of their own, Flamemaster Caydn, to take up the mantle of Sentry of the Order."

Kieran locked eyes with Caydn for a moment.

There's still something strange about him, Akiri.

"I agree," Akiri replied. "Though I sense no threat."

No, not a threat, Kieran agreed. *But something...*

"Last," Hartlan spoke on. "I would like to speak on the direction of the Academy as we move forward from this event. In this time, it is imperative that we remember the importance of our choices. We are all entrusted with unique gifts and abilities. We are, as we always have been, stronger when we are united. May we never forget that."

At last, Hartlan turned and exited the dining hall. Luri leaned in to Kieran.

"I wonder if the Order will truly stay away from the Academy now."

"Who knows," Kieran shrugged, taking another bite of his pastry.

After breakfast, Luri left to help Shivyn back to his room to rest. Kieran ducked out of the dining hall but found himself face to face with Artemael.

"Well, if it isn't the Midling himself," Artemael sneered.

"Go away, Artemael," Kieran warned angrily. He felt the familiar throbbing of magic in his chest.

"Or what? You'll send a giant flaming bird at me too?"

Kieran gritted his teeth. Artemael stepped closer.

"You'll regret what you've done to my family," Artemael hissed in Kieran's ear. "It's your fault my brother turned into a Wilder. I'll make sure that one day everyone knows what you really are."

Kieran's blood boiled as Artemael stormed off with his cronies. Kieran shook his head and thought back to the dragon egg.

I need you to trust me Akiri, because I'm about to do something stupid.

Chapter Twenty
Hidden Hope

"You were right," Akiri's voice echoed in Kieran's head. "You *were* about to do something foolish."

Kieran looked down at the jagged cliff-side below him. His breath came out in little puffs of fog. He reached out and pulled himself higher until he was at the top of the cliff.

Now, I just have to hike up the mountainside until I reach the nest.

Kieran trudged upward, panting. The cool air felt draining, and he almost longed to be back in the Ignis Lair.

At last, Kieran reached the summit and made his way toward the dragon's nest. It seemed more difficult to locate than the first time, and Kieran feared the egg might not still be there.

Kieran's fears were relieved when he finally spied the egg sitting squarely in the center of the nest. Kieran had brought a leather knapsack, and he gently picked up the egg to place it inside. He held the egg for a moment, feeling a warmth radiating from inside.

No one deserves to be left alone, Kieran thought as he lowered the egg into the sack.

Kieran returned from the mountain with no incident. He had irrationally feared that the dragon might return once he took the egg, but his fears proved unfounded.

Kieran made his way straight to his room when he arrived back at the Academy. He shut the door behind him and slowly pulled the egg from the knapsack.

"It should stay hidden," Akiri said. Kieran carefully placed it on a blanket and slid in beneath his bed.

The next few weeks passed uneventfully. Classes felt mundane after Kieran's battle with Kovesh. His schedule had been slightly rearranged, and Kieran was disappointed to see that the new Ignis leader had still not arrived. His Flame Arte classes turned into free periods that he typically spent traipsing around the grounds or discreetly checking on the egg. The egg stayed rather unchanging and Kieran began to wonder if perhaps it would hatch at all.

One exciting change was that Master Hartlan had finally been leading the Sunfire class. The old textbooks were promptly retired as Master Hartlan began walking them through the blended artes.

"As Sunfires, you have stepped past flame artes and have incorporated elements of earth magic as well," Hartlan said during class one day. "You will learn how to merge different artes together to wield more complex magic."

Kieran wondered if Hartlan was going to incorporate water artes as well, but he saw no indication that he would.

Akiri, do you think Hartlan will reveal that he's a Midling to the rest of the Academy?

"I do not know," Akiri replied. "It's hard to guess what another person will or won't do."

Kieran went back to practicing blending magic. Hartlan's tasks were easy if Kieran and Akiri brought their magical rhythms together. Still, when Kieran returned from class, he went straight back to his room. He felt exhausted.

Kieran plopped down on the bed and closed his eyes. Sleep started to overtake him, but then suddenly a slight scratching noise startled him.

What's that?

"The egg!" Akiri explained.

Kieran dove off the bed and into the floor. He pulled the egg carefully out and placed it before him. It gave a slight wiggle, and more scratching sounds were emitted.

Kieran watched in amazement as a tiny crack formed in the shell. Several more minutes of pecking and scratching ensued before the crack started to widen.

It's hatching! Kieran exclaimed to Akiri.

The egg tipped over on the floor and Kieran jumped. A tap from inside the egg helped bust the top of the shell open.

Out stumbled a coppery-red baby dragon. Kieran's eyes were wide as he watched the little dragonling take its first wobbly steps into the world.

"Hey there, little guy," Kieran held out his hand.

The dragon gave his hand a sniff, followed by a tiny little sneeze that nearly knocked it over. Kieran chuckled.

He kept his hand extended, and the little dragonling cautiously touched its scaly head to Kieran's palm. Kieran felt a leap of magic in his chest as the dragon's magic connected to Akiri.

The dragon let out a delighted little squeak and rolled over to his back. Kieran pet its belly and the dragon closed its eyes contentedly.

A sudden gasp from the doorway startled Kieran, and he looked up to see a horrified Luri staring at him and the dragon.

"Kieran! What have you done?"